PAST
HABITUAL

STORIES

ALF MAC-LOCHLAINN

PAST HABITUAL

STORIES

DALKEY ARCHIVE PRESS
Champaign / London / Dublin

Library of Congress Cataloging-in-Publication Data

MacLochlainn, Alf, 1926-
    Past habitual / Alf MacLochlainn. -- First edition.
        pages ; cm
    Summary: Childhood play, scarlet fever, a first kiss,
    befriending a Nazi spy--the narrative of Past Habitual
    roams through experiences both commonplace and
    formative, all under the uneasy canopy of wartime
    Ireland. Moving with ease between the voices of a young
    child, a German immigrant, an IRA member and
    colloquial chatter, MacLochlainn forms a web of
    interactions that lay out a century's tensions. A combina-
    tion of traditional prose, poetry, monologue and musical
    depiction, Past Habitual is an engaging and fascinating
    depiction of an Ireland struggling through the effects of
    war--both distant and on her doorstep.
    1. World War, 1939-1945--Ireland--Fiction.
    2. Ireland--History--20th century--Fiction. I. Title.
    PR6063.A25317P37 2015
    823'.914--dc23

                                        2014027952

Partially funded by a grant by the Illinois Arts Council,
a state agency

Past Habitual received financial assistance
from the Arts Council of Ireland.

www.dalkeyarchive.com

Printed on permanent / durable acid-free paper
Cover: design and composition Mikhail Iliatov

Table of Contents

A stitch in time

THE CLOCK IN THE TOWER over our office was huge. A man could stand upright inside it and wonder was the clunk-clunk in front of him or beside him or behind him and then he could look down and see in the pit, beside the ladder by which he had ascended, massive driving weights and the heavy bob at the foot of the pendulum, swinging back and forth, its rocker arm allowing the weight-driven wheels to pass clunkingly, one tooth at a time. It had been so surprising, the first time I had ascended that ladder. That had been at the invitation of the government contractor for clock-winding, anxious to impress a fresh young staff member in this small office.

In those days—how distant such a phrase makes those days sound—in those days every civil service office had an attendance book, and every officer had to sign each day, recording his time of arrival. A senior officer, allowing a few minutes grace for excusable late-coming, would check attendance and punctuality and draw a line; anyone signing after this drawn line was a late-comer and over-frequent 'lates' on the record of a new recruit would earn extension of the probationary period, reprimand, or other punitive measures in the arsenal of the dreaded establishment officer. And so, of course, every office had to have a clock. While some offices, run by whizz-kid ministers, were equipped with electric master and slave clocks, most ticked their way along in the staid nineteenth-century way of the British civil service. Just as the Corporation of Dublin continued to employ Poddle-watchers for decades, perhaps centuries, after the culverting of that innocent little stream had curtailed its flow, so the Department continued to seek and allot contracts annually for the winding of clocks in its offices.

And 'the Department' had been the Department of Agriculture and Technical Instruction, the only department in the gov-

ernment of Ireland under the British Raj. So not only the elderly
herald-painter and the elderly typist and the retired sergeant of
the Royal Irish Constabulary ordering his blue-rinsed visitors
about, but the old clock winder too maintained important conti-
nuities, ignoring minor interruptions such as rebellion and civil
war. Even to reach the bottom of that ladder was nerve-racking
enough. The office was located in a noble eighteenth-century
building surmounted by its clock tower and incorporating in its
lower reaches the stump of an earlier tower, perhaps the very bas-
tion which had earlier guarded the medieval entrance to the city.
The ascent of the inner tower was by a spiralling stairway, each
stone step cantilevered into the wall, with no support on the other end. Some of the stone steps — rough-hewn how many years
ago? — were showing definite signs of dipping towards the centre.

The wall, from which the steps were hung, was pierced at
ground level by passages, each about two yards long — that is, the
wall was about two yards thick — and one of those passages was
the main entrance to the building. In another, even in this short
length, there was a slight bend. To their surprise, visitors to the office were sometimes forced to demonstrate the defensive powers
of that doorway. It gave access to a museum, located in the ground
floor of the building and outside the original tower. It was the
practice of our ex-RIC man to adopt a hands-on approach to museum visitors and, brooking no denial, he would force a daughter
of the American Revolution to stand in the passage while he explained that the slight bend in it was the key to its ingenious defensive strength; for no right-handed wielder of a sword could get
a proper lead-in to thrust or swipe with his weapon, and thus a
defender had always the advantage of that few inches grace given
by the subtle bend in the passage. "Stand there now," he'd say, in
mellifluous Kerry tones, "and imagine you're defending the tower
against an attacker, that's me. You see how easy it is, I can't strike
a real blow at you."

Besides that Kerryman, a hang-over from the RIC, there was a
typist who, like the sergeant, was approaching retirement, whose
accent spoke more of Rathgar and the *ancien régime*. And in a

small room, almost an attic, at the last stop of those daintily-hung steps, there was an elderly scrivener. Perhaps illuminator would be a kinder word, for she was the last relic of a studio in which there had been produced the favourite testimonials of the late nineteenth century; the illuminated addresses presented to returning exiles who had struck it rich and were endowing charitable enterprises, or long-standing members of parliament, or scions of a landlord dynasty coming of age or bringing home a bride.

A yard-and-a-half of your best vellum, please. I'll pin it on my drawing board and damp it slightly, stretch and repin it again tomorrow. Eventually I'll have it as stretched as may be, limp and submissive, ready for the illuminator's pencil.

The texts, it goes without saying, were strings of honeyed epithets qualifying a handsome young scion of a noble house to whom the industrious peasantry his tenants were indebted for acts motivated by the highest principles ... But nobody read the text anyway, they just smirked proudly at being associated with something beautiful. And beautiful these illuminated addresses were, with faintly floral wreathings separating the paragraphs, pointillist dotted lines of scrolling, swirling zoomorphic flourishes highlighting the names of his honour and his bride, or his father, or whoever the grateful peasantry were kowtowing to on that particular occasion.

Our illuminator was finishing her last patent. *To all and singular*, it began, ... *greetings, whereas application hath been made unto me setting forth that* [name of applicant] *is desirous that certain armorial bearings as in the margin hereof more clearly depicted may be enrolled in the records of my office in the terms following* [a blazon of the arms] *as appertaining to him and to the heirs of his body lawfully begotten or to be begotten in accordance with the laws of heraldry ...*

Somewhere in the text, perhaps parallel to one of the swirling lines forming the name of the grantee, she would indict in tiny letters her name and the date. Then she would put away her inks and brushes, pens and scrapers, in the compartmentalised case in which they had entered the office fifty years before, and for the last time she would descend that stairway, with its steps slanting dangerously towards the vacant central void of the ancient tower.

The problem of replacing the retired herald-painter was not one for a junior recruit to the staff. And a problem it was. The market for illuminated addresses had dried up completely; calligraphy, even handwriting, was withering under the attack of peel-off, stick-on lettering, so there was no queue of applicants clamouring for a chance to blazon and emblazon arms as in the margin hereof more clearly depicted etc., etc. As for following precedent, the civil service standby—here there was no precedent. The old lady was, like so much else, a hangover from the old days, and was probably a product of some school for the daughters of distressed gentry, where suitable young ladies were instructed in useful and lady-like arts and crafts, then wafted quietly into posts at the disposal of various crown-appointed officers—oh forget it, the civil service didn't want to know, and a word to the head of the art college brought a young woman to our door, with a note from her professor saying he would suggest we interview her with a view to … etc. Which indeed we did. I say 'we', but of course it was my superior who did the interviewing and told me next morning that yes, we would be taking her on, and would I show her around, give her the necessary briefing? She was a tall willowy blonde who looked as if her silky grey top and wraparound skirt had been thrown at her and had stuck randomly, but her smile was ready and willing and she seemed genuinely interested in the job.

I had first to explain that, in such a small office with so few staff members and a begrudging attitude on the part of the Board of Works to an office they regarded as foreign, there was only one toilet, situated under the ogival arches in the basement, the stump of the original tower. I also had to teach her how to activate the flush, which required a nice balance of pull on chain; pause; release; pause; quick pull. To my surprise, none of this seemed to embarrass her.

"And how are you for scrivenry?" I asked, as we paused before a framed patent beginning with the florid *Georgius rex*.

"For what?" she said.

"You know," I said, "Scrivenry, writing, *scríobh* in Irish, inscribe in English. This heraldry is a funny language, mostly Norman French. You won't be writing, you'll be engrossing—*gros* is French for big or fat. The big black letters are French letters." She might well have permitted herself a snigger but she merely smiled, and I blundered on.

She knew nothing of heraldry so I, with an elementary knowledge of the subject, could pass myself off as an expert, remarking that a school badge with which she was probably familiar was fully and accurately described in the blazon *gyronny of eight argent and sable, a cross flory counterchanged.*

"People often talk of crests," I explained loftily, "when they really mean coats of arms. A coat of arms and a crest are parts of an achievement of arms, and not the only parts; there might also be a motto and supporters or a banner. The crest was the thing which the knight in armour had tied to his helmet, by a wreath, to make sure his own men recognised him in battle, and the wreath was of the same two colours as occurred in the coat itself."

"Never mind," she replied, in, as I realised to my shame, almost the first words I had given her a chance to contribute since we had begun the tour of the premises, "I'm sure I'll be able to get all that in a book. Of course I may have to report back to you for further toilet training. But wasn't this the building where the famous robbery took place years ago?"

"Yes indeed," I agreed, knowing that her very asking of the question put her in a one-up position when compared to someone who had joined the office before ever hearing a word about that scandal of ancient times. Recovering by repeating gossip gathered from the ex-RIC sergeant, I told her that the common belief was that it was well known who had taken the crown jewels, that the jewels were in the drawer of the table at which sat the commission of enquiry into the affair. "Bought back," the sergeant had said, "and we know who had the benefit of the purchase and managed to get off with himself to Canada, where he spent the rest of his life enjoying the handsome ranch he was able to buy."

"But why?" I had asked. And he explained that people in high places didn't want any light cast on goings-on by certain parties in the office and certain of their friends. And when I persisted with the question he had shrugged and contented himself with a two-word explanation: "Unnatural vice."

She again showed not the slightest embarrassment when I repeated this account of the most notorious event in the history of the office.

"What about timekeeping?" she asked, and I explained that she wasn't a civil servant, she would be paid on piece-work out of fees paid to the office, which were treated as appropriations in aid — her eyes began to betray a lack of attention and I explained more simply that she made her own times but would not be given a key, so would have to come and go by arrangement with some member of the established staff.

"What do you do about lunch?" was her next practical question, and I told her about the Castle lunch club, where clerks in dozens had sausage and mash followed by 'tappy and jam' and similar delightful grub for very reasonable charges. The sergeant made his own arrangements, I think a couple of pints in a snug nearby; the boss joined an old friend in the Dolphin; the elderly typist, who lived near a convenient bus-line, went home; and I brought a packed lunch and took it in the office.

"Nobody's clock-watching," I told her.

"This joint is out of time," she replied.

Next day at about one o'clock, as I opened the drawer of my desk to fetch out my thermos and sandwiches, the silence was broken by taps on my door, and our new herald-painter, Rebecca — that was her name — came hesitantly into my office, carrying the stout paper bag with folded-in top which I recognised as the equivalent of the traditional lunch-pail, and an *Irish Times* under her arm. "Do you mind?" she asked, "this place is a bit spooky on your own, maybe it's the ghost of Lord Haddo and his Hell Fire Club friends."

"I think you'd ha' been safe," I rejoined, "it's me that would have been at risk, but come in, come in, by all means."

So our lunch-hour became an appointment; for small-talk, inconsequential fragments of the morning's newspaper, with sidelong glances at various politicians in disgrace and mutual acquaintances in the world of the arts.

Not long after her arrival — the sun was high and gave a bright look to her top-floor 'studio' with its northern lighting — the clockman came again to do his duty and she confessed as she arrived for lunch that it had never occurred to her to wonder how the clock kept going.

"Come on, I'll show you." This invitation was no more than it says, another chance for me to show off. The ladder for access to the clock was hinged to fold back against the wall at the top end of that ancient but dodgy stairway.

"You may hear me complaining about the Board of Works," I said, "but they have their reasons. You may say 'overstaffed' and 'feather-bedding', and joke about the number of men, people, it takes to change a light-bulb, but let one person go up a ladder without a mate backing him up — as sure as God the bloody ladder will slip, with disastrous results, and why wasn't it secured? So I'll unhook this restraining loop and fold out the ladder, drop this bolt into place, muttering the magic words while you go up the ladder and open the trapdoor into the next storey above."

She nodded and put her foot on the first step. As I stood beside the ladder, holding tight to one rung, she mounted slowly and hesitantly, pausing when her hips were level with my face, so I became aware of a musky scent.

"OK?" I called, and shakily came the response:

"I'm not very good at heights, but I'll manage."

Another couple of rungs and her feet were in their turn level with my face and as I looked up to see how she was doing, I could see that the wraparound silky grey skirt she was wearing — very arty-crafty — had come loose as she stepped rung by rung. The tremor of her nervousness communicated itself through the solid wood. "OK?" I called again, and she looked down.

"OK yourself," she said, smiling, and reached out to open the trapdoor leading upwards.

I followed her up the ladder and accepted the hand she proffered in aid as I stepped off the top rung, one arm encumbered with the two packed lunches. Among the beams which supported the great wheels and spindles of the clockwork there was little room for lunchers, so we had to squat back-to-back on the floor. "*Addorsé*," she remarked, obviously beginning to master the terminology of our craft. Our talk and our meal was now punctuated by the clunk-slow-clunk of the escapement.

When we stood in the clock and looked out the narrow mullioned windows, we had a rare view of Dublin, or rather of that part of it which was over a certain height. The taller buildings stood proud of their neighbours, as adults might stand out among small children. We seemed to belong to a new and secret community at a higher level of being. Our only neighbours were our fellows in these tall buildings, rising out of amorphous anonymity. A phrase such as 'the lower orders,' which I would normally find hateful, seemed to me to describe the life and society we had left below among the 'ordinary people,' while we, floating in space up here, communed only with our companions of the upper reaches. There the big gasometer stood, beyond it the chimneys of the Pigeon House, nearby chimneys of the famous brewery and spires, domes and towers of medieval churches, St. Audoen's, St. Catherine's, even in the distance the slim column of the Wellington monument in the Phoenix Park. She expressed appropriate gratitude for this unusual view, taking my hand firmly in hers so that I might hand her down to the top rung of the ladder.

"Affrontant," she called out triumphantly a few days later, when I took up the squatting position facing her, to make conversation that bit easier. She was moving into the alphabet of terms but I was way ahead.

"Are you sure it's not an impalement?" I asked.

"Impaled like Vlad?" came her query, "that'd be horrible heraldry."

"No," I explained, "it's just when two coats are marshalled side by side they're said to be in pale ..." The air sometimes crackled with electricity, magnetism, static, I know not what, but the force exists in a still clarity of the atmosphere, carrying sound more clearly than usual, and setting aquiver little light hairs on the back of my neck. It is usually a presage of storm and thunder. One day from our eyrie in the clock-tower, we saw it happen. The sky's steely greys had clumped into towering black masses, standing out from a glittering white background. Lightning flickered around the edges of the black towers, then shot a jagged flash across the sky, with a shattering noise tearing the silence apart, as if a vast load of misshapen, hard-edged crates had been jumbled and tumbled together by giant hands and scattered on the floor of some resounding vestibule of hell above our heads. The first juicy drops of rain spattered against the clear glass of the clock-tower's narrow windows, and before the view was completely obscured by down-flowing rain we had a startling vision: those taller buildings, chimneys, domes, towers and spires, sharp-edged, holding their heads high, stood out from the murk of a low-lying mist, saluted one another, islands of an archipelago in the filmy darkness.

"Oh jeez," Rebecca almost moaned, visibly shivering, "I can't stand thunder."

Surprised, I tried to reassure her: "It's going to be OK, there's no danger—come on, we'll go down now."

I reached out to take her hand and felt in it the tremor of her nervousness. Holding my hand she drew herself to me, then locked her arms round my neck and kissed me violently. I knew now one reason for her tremor at the sudden drop in temperature—under the silky top which complemented the arty-crafty wraparound flowing skirts she favoured, she was wearing nothing, and the silvery grey silk was no barrier to the signs of passion in her embrace. Which I returned.

Demolition of a gnome-house

THERE WAS ALWAYS AN ENVELOPE. If I had been old enough to speak like my older brothers I would have said there was always a bloody envelope and I was pretty damn sure it was about money. An envelope either in my mother's hand or my uncle's. My uncles came visiting much more after my Dada died. Sometimes my Grandpapa, who had a stick, walked all the way from Rathmines.

I went into the parlour where my mother and my uncle were. I wanted to show them my gnome-house. I did not know what a gnome was but I knew how to make a gnome-house. I was in town with my mother and one of my big brothers before that, maybe a week before, but anyway after my other uncle had called, and we were getting shoes for my big brother. We believed that it was bad for new shoes to give them their first wearing in wet weather but the afternoon was fine and my brother badly wanted to wear his new shoes right away so he was let put them on and the old pair were put in the box. As soon as we got home I asked for it. Next morning I threw away the lid and tore off the end with the label on it and went out to the back garden to find a good place for my gnome-house.

I don't know how big the garden was, but if I rushed out the back door it did not take many steps to bring my outstretched palms slap against the rough rubble of the end wall. Those few steps had taken me past my mother's flower-bed on one side, a lean-to scullery, a coal-house, and a lav on the other, then past a lilac tree and a couple of wrinkled apple-trees facing a patch of bare clay. No grass grew on the clay there; we played cricket and hurling on that patch and from a garden so few steps long the ball was often canted over the wall into Masson's nursery next door. The wall was a good deal higher than a seven-year-old boy and we could climb over it only at a low place where a few stones had fallen off the top. Our hands could reach up and grasp nice rounded stones up high while the soles of our shoes scraped for support on the rough edges of yellow stones with shiny flakes in them near the bottom. We could nearly always get our ball back without getting a chase from the man in the nursery. Our garden was enclosed by this wall and the high brick wall of the nursery's stable with its loft. We could smell the horses and the hay. And we sometimes had rats! From the stable, my mother said.

Halfway down the garden there was a fence of rusty chicken-wire to protect my mother's flowers from the ball-playing beyond, and on the ground, at the beginning of the bare clay, and nearly at the middle point of the whole garden, I placed my shoe-box, upside down, and knelt beside it. With its floor now serving as roof, its sides as walls, and the gap of the torn-off end as a doorway, it already looked a bit like a house. It still smelt of leather and cardboard, and hard edges of shiny white paper, still showing, were wrong, wrong for a gnome-house, so I ran about the garden collecting bits of grass and weeds from the untrodden margins by the walls. I heaped them over the upturned box and sprinkled grey clay on top. Now it blended better into the garden and began to be a proper house. To make it into a gnome-house I had to build paths to it and around it and for these I needed fragments of broken delph. We were a family of rough boys and the rate of breaking was high, so it did not take me long to find a few dozen fingernail-sized bits of broken crockery, white or blue or pink. I pressed them in lines into the clay, marking little pathways to the door of the gnome-house and around its walls. Even when it was finished I had no sense that there could ever be a gnome living in it. I did not know what a gnome was: some sort of fairy, perhaps, and a fairy I could imagine from pictures in books; or a leprechaun maybe — but I never believed in those things, even in my earliest childhood.

"Couldn't you go and play outside for a while?"

I knelt in front of the finished gnome-house and bent low so that I could peer into the dark inside. There was still the smell of leather and cardboard but it was mingled with the sneezy dust off the clay and the spiced sharpness of broken dandelion leaves and stems. Their tacky white ooze on my fingers had the dust stuck all over it and my hands were filthy.

"Would you run over and get a pennyworth of pot-herbs for the soup for dinner from Miss Crosbie at the vegetable counter in Findlater's, there's a good boy."

Findlater's was in the row of shops along one of the three sides of Sandymount Green; it was beyond Leman's the cobblers, beyond McDonnell's dairy. The vegetable counter was the first on the left as you entered the main shop — main shop because there was a rack of produce displayed outside, under an awning which was rolled, as weather required, in and out of a large slot above the double windows.

There were four counters altogether, two on the left, two on the right. The long open floor between them led towards the back of the shop, where there was a tall glass box with a lady sitting inside it. Wire tracks just below the ceiling ran from each of the counters to this box. When I gave Miss Crosbie the three-penny bit for the pennyworth of pot-herbs, she put it with a little slip of paper into a corrugated wooden jar, screwed a brass lid on the jar, and, reaching up, pushed it into a clip on the wire track. She gave a quick tug to a hanging handle and, with a twang and a snap, the jar shot off along the wire to the lady in the glass box. The change was sent back to Miss Crosbie with another hiss of the jar along the wire.

I knew about money, I could go for the messages.

"A half-pound of butter please."

At the second counter on the left the heap of butter lay on a marble slab behind Mr. Kennefick, where it had been slipped from the slope-sided butter-box with 'Irish creamery butter 56 lbs' burnt or stamped in brown on the smooth white wood. With stabs of his sharp wooden pats, Mr. Kennefick chopped off lumps as required. He jabbed and slapped with the ridged paddles and cut out a piece which he landed on the square of grease-proof paper lying ready on the tray of his weighing scales. Deft taps made it into a neat oblong block, and it weighed exactly half a pound.

The paper was lapped over, the ends beyond the butter folded in and turned up against the square ends of the oblong, the whole then slipped into a brown paper bag.

"A pound of sugar, please."

At the third counter, to the right at the back of the shop, the sugar was in a huge bin with a sloping lid. I was lucky, there were no filled bags standing waiting on the shelf behind. Mr. Duffy flipped up the lid of the bin and shoved in a wide scoop which came up filled with the glistening white crystals. He tipped just enough into a black paper bag standing ready on one tray of his scales to tip up the squat black weight on the other. The bag was firmly tied with white twine.

We never did business at the fourth and last counter: I call it last. I stood resolutely with my back to it as I faced Miss Crosbie, I knew that behind me were stacked boxed biscuits and chocolates, packaged cakes, in front of them a terraced rampart of biscuit boxes, their hinged glass lids displaying their attractions. My face firmly set towards Miss Crosbie and her tiered punnets of carrots, lettuce, beans and peas in their pods, fronted by bigger trays of cabbage and turnips, small and white or purple and Swede, flanked by earth-smelling sacks of potatoes. Miss Crosbie weighed potatoes in a big sideways bucket a bit like the coal-bucket we had beside the fire at home, and, swinging the bucket skilfully, she shot the potatoes from its rolled-tip mouth into the customer's shopping bag.

"And the pennyworth of pot-herbs, please."

Behind me, unmentioned, reared the mountain of forbidden delights: cakes, sweet biscuits, chocolates.

"A pound and a half of lean round steak for stewing."

This from Mr. Sheils, whose butcher's shop was on Seafort Avenue, just round the corner from the Green. (That was the Ryan's pub corner, where the young men stood, with their backs to the iron bar protecting the window-sill.) Shiels's shop was opened to the wide air, by the sliding up of ribbed black shutters. There was sawdust all over the floor and there was a door in the corner which was the entry—or so it was said—to the slaughter-house, where the real butchery was done. Certainly the great yellow bulk of meat was not to be recognised as any part of any animal as it thudded onto the chopping block hewn from the whole trunk of a tree. Mr. Shiels's knife, worn narrow and thin with sharpening, hung in a wooden scabbard at his side. He reached across the half carcase and with his knife pierced and slit it, slicing evenly and smoothly, baring the inner redness, down to the bone. A scrape with a saw, and a chop through the bone with a cleaver, and there on the block lay a wide slab of meat, a round eye of bone and marrow in the centre. When he had cut off and weighed the half pound I had asked for, he threw on the scales beside the meat a lump of crinkly white fat.

There was a tangy smell from my hands when I got home. The strong sweet smells of sage and thyme mingled on the fingers which had clutched them all through that long list of messages, mingled as they would in the soup, with the musky blood-stained smell of the bullock's yellow corpse.

Oh I knew about money alright, even if that day's sending for just a pennyworth of pot-herbs was some kind of trick. And when they said "Why don't you go and play outside?" did they mean in the back garden, or on the wide pavement outside the front door, or even farther away, on the strand? I went to the strand by myself sometimes, but only when I was let specially. It was two hundred and five running paces away, I had counted it, panting, and pausing for safety before the final dash across Strand Road. "And don't come home on the narrow side but be careful crossing." The narrow path was round the corner from our house, between the high garden wall of a big house and the tramtracks. Big boys stood deliberately on this narrow path to show their nerve as trams swayed by but I was a little afraid of the clanking bulks with their trolleys singing on the high-hung wires overhead.

I could turn a sand-castle into a tar-melting works. I bored a little tunnel from the side into the centre of the castle and then poked a little chimney to the top. I put the butt of a candle in the dark middle under the chimney and above it a cocoa-tin lid filled with tar picked sun-softened from between the setts of the tramway. Lighting the candle was never easy, in the breeze which always blew gently across the strand, but when it lit and stayed alight, the tar soon began to bubble. Flow ran crazily between the ribs and into the runnels left by the last ebb, filled the moat around the castle, ran into the candle's cave, quenched the flames, wore away the whole structure and knocked down and resolidified the bubbling black tar. We pranced around in our bare feet, shouting glee and encouragement to the tar and the tide.

Digging in the sand made my hands clean, while scraping paths to and around my gnome-house turned the spaces under my fingernails into black rims; but the gnome-house lasted. I knelt again before it and bowed low to peer in. It was dark in there. The low afternoon sunlight, slanting over the nursery wall, glinted off broken china and cast a few faint gleams inside.

I had a horrid dream last night which may have had its beginning in my hard peering into my little house. We had a baby, my wife and I, perhaps not biologically ours, just with us, a tiny baby, not much more than newborn, though with a thatch of black hair. There were three separate scenes in my dream. First the baby, merely present. Then, the baby with an ugly black ulcer disfiguring its forehead. Then, the horrid part — there was a hole as big as half a crown in the baby's upper forehead. I could look in and see the inside surface of its hollow skull, with something shining like silver paper at the bottom of the dark cavity. The infant's tiny fingers were reaching up and picking at the proud edges of the hole. The thick mat of hair was gone. From large patches of bare skin a few odd hanks were hanging down.

I put my face beside the doorway and smelt the damp cardboard. I knew that in the front parlour they were saying things they did not want me to hear because there were things they did not want me to know, probably about money. My eyes smarted with tears because I could not imagine what kind of things such things might be.

The star-crystal of a tear in my eye magnifies the dark doorway of my gnome-house and I stamp my foot in rage and frustration and march in. I look round at my handiwork, the high dark brown walls. I look back through the doorway at the grey dusty clay of the sunlit garden. I smell the piled earth and withering grass of the roof.

I know the way to the shops and I can buy the messages. I know how far it is to the strand and how to get back safely. I can build a house with walls and a roof and coloured paths to it and around it, but there are unnameable things away above and beyond. The solid universe lies unchartable before me and I stand up to the full height of a seven-year-old boy. Through the tears streaming from my eyes I can barely see the collapsing gnome-house as it falls in ruins in the dust about my feet.

The minstrel boy

BOOM-bang-a-bang DOOM-bang-a-bang BOOM-bang-a-bang
Clatter-te-tattle-te-rattle-te-tattle-te-tee TING TING

DOOM-bang-a-bang BOOM-bang-a-bang DOOM Clatter-te-
rattle-te-tattle-te-tee Ting-TING

Short trousers knee socks Short trousers knee socks TING TING
Pursed lips blow hard pursed lips blow hard

Eyes front fingers on holes PIPING FIFING TING TING
The short trousers were scratchy, what'd you expect? Bang TING

The coarse wool torn from the barbed wire up the farm, TING
bang

Rust and raddle and Christ knows what mixed with it

DOOM-bang FIFING PIPING

In came the captain's daughter BANG TING Or even when shorn
from the sheep up the mountain TING ting

Carded spun and woven and cut Clatter-te-rattle-te-tattle-te-tee
TING TING

Cut and sewn in the workshop-stop TING TING

And dress myself in man's attire DOOM .... BANG .... TING

Lift foot left foot marking time MARK TIME

Step together, *to the war has gone*

His father's sohord he has girded on TING TING

BOOM bang-a-bang *slung behihind him*

Out from the shadow of the stand BOOM BANG

Land of song TING TING

All the world betrays BANG Bang fife whines

Lookit the crowd in the stand BOOM TING

Right turn, blue cape swirling TING BOOM

Harp shall praise thee clatter-a-tee

TINGBOOM WHINE

BOOM-bang-a-bang DOOM

Never brought his proud soul under THUNDER

Clatter-te-tatter-te-tatter-te-tatter-te-tee TING TING

BOOM-bang-a-bang latter-day-clatter-day-Saturday TING TING

If we'd only ha' knowin' about that

It was cats on one side looking like wasps

In their striped black and amber,

And on the other an *urbs intacta*

Years and years ago.

Don't you know your Latin, boy? D'you serve Mass? Yes. Sir,

Ad Deum qui laetificat juventutem meum

Dom 'scum

'sti tuo amen.

But I don't know any of those words in the Mass sir.

How old are you boy?

Thirteen sir.

Well it's time you knew some of these things, when class is over go
to that big dictionary on the shelf there and tell me tomorrow what
intacta means

Seven feet is his height with some inches to spare Bang boom
One two wait for the DOWN BEAT five BOOM boom
No no stop, you're blowing like hissing geese

SMOOTH, now again, you boy, with the triangle,
follow the beats

The rest of you TING you come in on the down beat,

One two watch it now ting

To the war has gone

War has gone SHRILL SHRILL

BOOM bang a bang BOOM

BOOM-bang-a-bang DOOM Clatter-te-rattle-te-tattle-te-tee
TING TING

BOOM-bang-a-bang BOOM Clatter-te-rattle-te-rattle te TING-
BOOM BOOM

It was in the interval between the minor and the senior hurling finals in the great stadium that the band from the industrial school
strutted their stuff. There were about forty boys in the band—
about, because the number could fluctuate with the fancy and
temper of the brother in charge. Five rows of eight made a brave
show, in their short blue capes, fifes squeaking, as if to substitute
for the breaking treble voices of the pubertal marchers. The big
drum to the rear of the formation beat a heavy rhythm, BOOM
DOOM boom boom kettle-drums rattled and the triangles erect
on frames, rang out high-frequency pulses to establish the length
of the marching steps ting ting piping fifing whine
  "Now where's our young Latin scholar—there, did you look
that up?"
  "Yes sir, intact means unbroken."
  "So it does boy, and did the book tell you anything about *urbs
intacta*?"
  "No sir."

"Well I'll tell you because there's a big hurling match coming on next Sunday and you may bet that Micheal O Hehir, if he's doing it on the radio, will say something about *urbs intacta*, because that's what Waterford likes to call itself. Way back in history when the English claimed to be entitled to boss Ireland whatever way they liked, there was a row going on about who should be king of England, and the main guy claiming it was opposed by two others one after the other, they were called Lambert Simnel and Perkin Warbeck, and there was lots of chieftains in Ireland who were delighted to support them, for the sake of having a go at the sitting king, but not Waterford, the fat business men in Waterford stayed loyal to Richard and for this they got called intact, unbroken."

Then turning to me, "You'll remember that boy, even if it wasn't in the book? And did it say anything about *virgo intacta*?"

I blushed and stammered. "Yes sir."

"Well come to my room after class and I'll explain it to you ..."

after class after Mass *and other wicked spirits who wander through the world for the ruin of souls*

We were going on from sums to arithmetic and geometry and an ordinary man, a layman, came in to teach us mathematics. It's all so many years ago that I've forgotten all the stuff about 'a' standing for any number and 'b' standing for any other number and 'ab'—oh never mind, but what I do remember is that he was interested in the hurling match too and told us why the Kilkenny team that was going to play Waterford were called the cats: the Kilkenny cats in the old story were so vicious with one another that they et one another alive and there was nothing left.

Forty years after, almost to the day, allowing for the fact that the big match is on the first Sunday in September, the whole sorry story was paraded across the tabloids, and got fair coverage in the broadsheets too. Autumn 1998, and people were much readier now to make accusations against agencies of Holy Mother Church. In the old days you wouldn't dare say a word against anything religious, but now there was a raft of people making allegations against twenty members of the community which ran that school.

> *A song for the Pope for the royal Pope,*
> *Who rules from sea to sea,*
> *Whose kingdom or sceptre never shall fail,*
> *What a grand old king is he is he,*
> *What a grand old king is he.*

Some of the accusers had been in the band with me and were about the same age, say about sixty, when we made the complaint, or about ten or twelve in the late fifties when we marched round the stadium playing 'The Minstrel Boy' as the hurling teams of Kilkenny and Waterford stood around flexing their muscles and waiting to be photographed before the big match. And the other patriotic tunes as well—'Kelly, The Boy from Killane,' 'The Boys of Wexford,' 'Ireland Boys, Hurray' Bang Bang.

Even 'The Boys from the County Cork' got a blast now and again but for a change it wasn't the boys from the County Cork that year; Soldiers of the legion of the rearguard, more like. The name of the school had been changed but there was no mistaking the faces, splashed in photographs on the tabloids, part obscured by a raised arm or a hand before the eyes and nose, and grown haggard.

Pay them all back the deep debt so long due Crattle-te-rattle TING DOOM *Give them back blow for blow*

The school had only an oratory, the Blessed Sacrament was not reserved there, and the outside of its end wall, emblazoned with an emblem in moulded concrete, frowned down on a public street. Passersby late at night, or early morning milkmen, might occasionally hear the crying of small boys coming from windows which shared that wall with an embossed star, a scroll above it proclaiming the name of the religious society within, and a scroll below with the inscription *Signum fidei.*

Signum fidei indeed, the other early morning sound was perhaps another and equally ironic sign of faith, the clatter of wooden-soled clogs as the boys in a troop were herded to fields in the outer suburbs, where they toiled in the cold and damp, thinning

turnips or cabbages or digging potatoes as the seasons might dic-
tate. The clogs, like the tweed suits, were produced in the institu-
tion's workshops, where the boys were notionally being trained in
useful skills, though nowhere else in the whole of Ireland were
clogs like those to be seen — or heard. Boys passing out from the
school to take some kind of place in the real world got rid of the
coarse suits as quickly as they possibly could, as a frightened Jew
in Nazi Germany might have hoped to get rid of the star which
marked him as despised victim of brutal and evil power.

The boys who were selected for training as band boys were
spared some of the tasks which might have damaged their hands,
and some of the routine punishments. Instead they were drilled
repeatedly by supervisors or instructors who took full advantage
of the close indoor confinement which the music teaching required or permitted. Cruel older boys who had suffered themselves assured the younger that they would be taught the flute and
the French horn. And those older boys cackled with laughter as
their juniors struggled to extract some meaning from the cryptic
advice.

The cases dragged on and on, and people got fed up with reading that statements were made by complainants who couldn't be
named for legal reasons and of accused who remained nameless to
protect their victims; but in those victims there remained a glow-
ing fire within. *Give them back blow for blow* Boom Bang clatter-
te-ting The school's name had been changed and what had been
the oratory became a dusty store. There were a few pews or forms
or benches shoved in a corner, cobwebs obscuring the carved ini-
tials of boys long gone. Less dusty, some in cases, some naked as
they were born, the band's instruments — French horns, fifes,
flutes, kettle drums, triangles — were stored on shelves of rough
deal planking, behind a small low thicket of foldable or clip-on
music-stands.

BOOM bang a bang, boom bang a bang, cattle te lattle te lattle
te lattle TING TING

Come the fiftieth anniversary of that encounter between the
mutually destroying cats and the intact youth of the other side,

heralded by the BOOM rattle TING of the boys' marching band, there was still no sign of movement in the case.

Why do we measure longer periods of time in even decades, centuries? The tenth anniversary of this, that, and the other is commemorated in the press, never the ninth or the seventh. Try the fiftieth—this gets to us, we want to mark it some way.

There was something repellent about the abandoned oratory. The air had a stale deconsecrated smell, the smell of the real absence, and anyone prepared to walk quietly and scramble over a few low walls could readily gain access to that former place of prayer at any time of day or night. The fact that the instruments were there was a pure bonus, and I conclude by quoting the *Irish Times* of September 8, 2008. The off-lead is the story of the hurling final, *Awesome Kilkenny seize the day* ..., the centre-piece of page 4 is a photograph of the flames engulfing the chapel of the former industrial school, and the attached story is headed *FIRE GUTS HISTORIC CHURCH USED FOR PRACTICE BY BAND.* One resident said that since the gates of the school are left open practically twenty-four hours a day, 'she was absolutely convinced the fire was started deliberately ...'

The rule of three

Multiplication is vexation
Subtraction is as bad
The rule of three perplexes me
And fractions drive me mad.

I ONCE WROTE A BOOK which was built on sets of four. When it was published, many of my friends were kind enough to say they enjoyed it and the few critics who noticed it found some merit in it. And nobody, but nobody, noticed the sets of four which I had so carefully used as the scaffold to support the structure of that story. It consisted of four linked short stories, and north, south, east and west featured, as did spring, summer, autumn, winter; spades, hearts, clubs, diamonds; and morning, afternoon, evening, night. Come to think of it, the image I have just used should have occurred to me before—scaffolding. The scaffolding, after all, is designed to finish up as an invisibility. It is there to support the building workers while building is in progress, and to be removed when the job is done. On the poured concrete of a *Unité d'Habitation* the imprints of the shuttering planks abide as testimony that someone was here, the joiners who knocked the shuttering together, the people mixing and pouring the concrete. In a distant view of the apartment block, we do not see them. Similarly, my story is held together by obvious threads such as the progressing of the plot, as well as by the less obvious, those sets of four, for example, and I should be flattered that my friends saw the story as the whole it was meant to be, rather than the accumulation of bricks, thumb-printed as the wet clay was fed laboriously into the kiln.

I wrote another story, and few of the readers seemed to realise that they were, so to speak, getting two stories for the price of one. This time, the story was built around twenty or so short indented paragraphs, typographically distinct from the main text. The main text told a story of the narrator and his father, who was a contributor to reference works, and the interpolated paragraphs, in reference-book style, and in alphabetical order, told a quite different story—in fact a parody of the Irish Big-House socially conscious narrative, complete with clerical crime and blackmail. And again, nobody saw it, though there were clues a-plenty.

This time I am confessing at the beginning that this whole narrative is based around sets of three, and I don't care whether that would have become obvious or not—three hours agony, say, or Hail Mary for your penance, coins in fountain, feet in yard, leafed clover, and so on, as will be made clear hereafter.

Joyful Mysteries

Misuse of words has always annoyed me (and by misuse I mean usage different from my own). Take the special vocabulary of boys contesting the relative strengths of their chestnuts. The school year began with the autumn term and its tedium was relieved by exploitation of the chestnut harvest. The mature nuts, shiny brown eyes with white pupils, were knocked from their parent trees with well-aimed sticks thrown from below. The spiky green pods, if truly ripe, would burst on hitting hard ground and reveal the rich brown nuts within, cased in white undergarments. (If you lost patience at the slow progress of the year and went harvesting chestnuts before they were properly mature, the pods would prove difficult to open and the aborted nuts within would be soft, and patchy pie-bald white and brown.) A hole was pierced through a likely nut and a foot or so of good twine passed through it, with a lumpy retaining knot at one end to prevent the nut's falling off.

The duel opened with a hurriedly shouted challenge— 'hickhack first crack.' The rejoinder of one accepting the challenge might be a half-friendly 'off your chest' (thump) 'nut' (thump), that is, with thumps to the chest and head; then the hand was held out gripping the string, with the provocative target nut dangling below. He with the first crack wound one end of his string around the fingers of one hand, while two fingers of the other hand, the string passing through the space between, restrained the nut and made a sight, as it were, of a cross-bow or firearm. The string was held thus, taut between two hands in line, pointing like an arrow at the target; a quick forward and downward flick of the wrist as the fingers behind released the nut, sent it whirling in an arc through the air, hopefully to expend is centrifugal energy by crashing into the dangling target opposite. It was a matter of honour to keep the target nut steady and unjiggling. The assailant either struck or missed his target, and became target in his turn. So turn and turnabout until one of the nuts was smashed, its shell burst open and the pale yellow kernel crumbled.

The victor now added one to the number of his earlier triumphs, if any, and indeed if his victim had earlier victories to his credit, the victor could add these too. Thus if a 'conqueror of three' overcame a 'conqueror of five', it became a conqueror of nine (think about it). There was no independent audit of these figures. And in the matter of the misuse of terms, the commonplace 'conker' for 'chestnut' is merely an uncouth perversion of the technically correct 'conqueror', which is always to be preferred.

Tanglers three

A defeated schoolfellow once claimed sulkily that his opponent had loaded a real steel nut, like off a bicycle axle, into a chestnut shell. Quite impossible, I realised later, but often rumoured of an unpopular victor claiming a high score. Far-sighted youths could achieve almost the hardness of steel by seasoning their weapons. A nut was peeled and pierced and placed in some nook or cranny adjacent to a fire-place. It became shrivelled and hardened and emerged a year later as a 'seasoner,' fit to take on all customers. Unless, perhaps, you had, like a squirrel, forgotten where you put it, or had passed on to the higher state of male teenage testosterone.

But tanglers three? If the assailant conq'rer missed the target nut by crossing the strings, the force of the blow would cause the nuts to whirl, orbiting each other, entangling the strings. He who first noticed this and cried 'tanglers three' earned a bonus of three uninterrupted attempts at striking the opponent's nut, now a hapless victim.

They say a moth clearing its throat in the Faroe Islands can by ripple, eddy, and chaos theory cause a tidal wave drowning thousands on the shores around the Indian Ocean. While Hitler was planning murder on an unimaginable scale and having his pliant minions organise it as the main industry of his 'Third Reich,' and Churchill was ordering his pikemen to the south coast of England to repel boarders, neither of them spared a thought for the cultural effect their wars of offence and defence were going to have on distant schoolboys in Rathmines.

The German U-boat attacks caused a severe shortage of British shipping, and native British heavy industry, transport, and power generation demanded massive supplies of fuel. Churchill allowed just a little to neutral Ireland, in return for information about weather, and about intercepts of largely pointless messages passing among the ill-briefed Germans sent to Ireland as spies and/or contacts with the relentlessly anti-British faction of the Irish Republican movement.

The upshot of the whole thing was that gas and electricity in Ireland were in very short supply and their use was rationed either by quantity or time of use. Gas was very generally used in Dublin and was available only during certain hours of the day. And—we'll get there, don't worry—to convenience as many people as possible by having whole households free for a daily main meal at the same time, the horarium of schools, and perhaps business as well, was changed. Our school day, which had previously run from half-past nine in the morning until three in the afternoon, with a short midday break, under the new gas-rationing regime was broken into two periods, half-past nine until half-past twelve and two o'clock until four o'clock. Under the earlier regime, I had brought a sandwich with me to school and gobbled it during the short break at noon, before plunging into energetic games around the school playground. Then I had been given

my dinner on my return home at half-past three or thereabouts. Now,
I cycled home and joined my elder brothers, all the family in fact, for
a full midday meal at about one o'clock. So far not much sign of the
Great Powers interfering with my cultural life?

Caught-locket one-two-three

But yes, for they put an end to the rough and tumble games
which had filled that half-hour in the school playground and had
filled the rooms for our afternoon classes with a reek of boyish
sweat. There were some sedentary games, of course; the more stu-
dious amongst us might take pencil and paper to a quiet corner of
the back field and engage in word-play games, or battleship spot-
ting. Our fleets consisted of blocks on gridded paper (our 'sum
copies'). Turn and turnabout, each of the two contestants fired off
a salvo at the unseen enemy, by calling out co-ordinates, column
and row, of the notional rounds it was hoped would reveal the
disposition of the rival naval forces. The victim of that salvo reported the fall of shot and in his turn fired off his salvo ...

But the many rushed about at relievio: chasing, catching, drag-
ging to incarceration in a den. You were not fairly caught unless your
captor managed to hold you long enough for him to gabble the formu-
la 'caught-locket one-two-three.' From the den you might be released
if one of your team could enter and leave it without being caught,
shouting 'relievio!' as he dashed through.

Three and in

At a certain age, relievio became childish in teenage eyes and
we graduated to a recognisable form of football. It was played by
pairs. One boy and his partner were goalies, the rest also formed
partner pairs, and each pair tried to outwit the others, gain possession of the ball and score a goal. When a pair had done this
successfully three times, they became the goalies — and so on.

Marbles, too, which had featured in our third or summer
term, we had left behind with the rest of our school-yard culture,
when that hectic midday break was abolished for us by Hitler and
his warmongering. (Mind you, I am not pretending that his sins

against Rathmines school-boys ranked high on the indictment when he was hauled before the Judgement Seat—and sentenced, I have no doubt, to a blistering eternity in an entirely appropriate crematorium.)

There were three sorts of marbles. The old-fashioned white plaster or plaster-plus job became eroded quickly into an ellipsoidal rather than spherical shape and rolled crazily and disobediently to left or right of its intended trajectory. It was therefore considered to be nothing better than poor white trash and was displaced by marbles of coloured glass, which came in two sizes. In clear glass spheres, the manufacturers had managed to incorporate bright swirls of colour and still succeeded in selling them very cheaply—a cardboard tube containing a dozen or so sold for a few pence. These were the common currency of marbles players, whose ambition always was to own at least one of the third and best kind—steel ball-bearings from the ball-races of heavy vehicles, true and enduring in their travel, and capable of overcoming obstacles of tufted grass or fallen lunch-crusts, which would have diverted the lighter glass specimens. These 'steelers' or 'ballers,' as they were called, were so highly valued that a convention had become established concerning their status in competition. Normally, if you lost a game, the marble you were playing with was forfeited, and became a trophy for the victor. But a player using a steel baller could, in the course of play, stipulate that if he lost the game it was not his prized baller that he would forfeit, but a run-of-the-mill glass stand-in.

The games too were of three sorts. Simplest was a tiny copy of ten-pin bowling, and it had the advantage that it could be played indoors. Players each contributed one to a spaced line of marbles which was formed near to and parallel with a wall. From an agreed base-line, perhaps across the room from the line, competitors rolled their marbles at this line, winning those they managed to strike out of it. Simplest of the outdoor versions was that begun with the formula 'folly on the whole way,' as a challenger's marble was rolled forward along the gutter, perhaps, between footpath and roadway. The third game was a miniaturised version

of something between golf, croquet and snooker. Three shallow
pits, let's say fist-sized, were dug in a straight line, a couple of feet
apart, and the one nearest an agreed start-line about a yard from
that line. Players had to roll their marbles successfully into those
holes in succession, with the right, en route, to strike opponents'
marbles into less favourable positions. Hole and taw, we called it,
though the word taw, fairly standard English for a marble, was
otherwise unknown to us.

Though there was no official promulgation or announcement
appointing a special day, the marbles, like so many other features
of life, belonged to a specific season, a part of the trimestrial, tri-
partite year, which all schoolboys recognised and observed. Other
seasonalities had more rational explanations. Cricket, for example, if it was played at all, was played in the spring-to-summer
term. At earlier periods, those flannelled fools at the wicket or the
idlers lounging about in the field in light white shirts would have
caught their deaths of cold; and the muddied oaf at the goal was
usually swaddled in garments which could maintain their heat for
an hour or longer.

The same summer term which saw cricket make some show,
also saw, on the serious side, boys in the fourth and sixth years of
their secondary schooling grinding hard for the major public ex-
ams. In accordance with ancient wisdom these were held late May
to early July. When we were in fifth year, therefore, we were enjoying the freedom which is nowadays experienced in what is
called a gap year. We were in a position to get ahead of those un-
fortunates still stuck in examination halls. They were important
to us in other ways — they had sisters. And we had learnt to sy-
chronise our comings and goings with those of the sisters.

That same pressure of war-time — sorry, emergency — shortages meant that there was no long-haul commuting to school; everything was intimate and local, and the bicycle reigned supreme.
Infants started with trikes, progressed to fairy cycles. If we were
going to the nearest secondary school, on our bikes, of course, our
sisters were going to the nearest secondary school for girls, or the
convent as we would familiarly say. And if our sisters were going

there so were our classmates' sisters, and a perfectly normal call on a classmate was, purely by chance of course, an ideal opportunity for making the acquaintance of—put it either way—our classmates' sisters, or our sisters' classmates. And it could happen that the class-mate on whom you called might not be at home, but his sister might be there, and she might even need some show of gallantry on the part of her brother's classmate, a little help perhaps with a bicycle repair. "Could we try it now?" asked with a fluttering of teenage eyes, led to a pleasant spin on leafy suburban roads and a proud sense of achievement.

Three speed gear

There is an interesting contrast and comparison to be drawn between bicycles and, of all things, stools. Start with the simplest proposition, geometrically speaking. A point is just a point, a location in universal space. But two separate points define a line, and a straight line is the shortest distance between two points. Add a third point, not on that line or any extension of it, and by lines joining each of your three points to the other two, you have defined a space, and this space establishes, defines, a plane. That space, that plane, doesn't have to be limited to lines joining three points, it might be four or five ... any number. When you join each of your points to each of the others, you are left with a strange mess—the outer perimeter is clear, you have a four-sided or five-sided figure, or whatever, depending on the number of points you're using, but internally it is a multiplicity of three-sided figures, triangles, and this no matter how many sides the outer perimeter has.

And it gets worse. Take a point which is not in the same plane as our original space, imagine lines from this outside point to each of those other points down there on that plane, and what have we described? Some kind of pyramid or crystal—with triangular facets. And again no matter how many sides, facets, you build up, it will always be possible to slice it into four-sided fractions with three triangular facets. Impossible to avoid the conclusion that there is a continuum—point, line, flat space, bulk vol-

ume … one, two, three, four points. What is the next item in this
series? Probably something to do with time … logical to ask what
where and when. And of course the continuum works the other
way too, and what is the end after point, a point being so unimag-
inably tiny that it has disappeared into its own infinitesimality?
Berkeley lost patience with the proponents of the infinitesmal.
They claimed that if you subdivided, for example, the circumference of a circle into millions of tiny arcs, each the 'size' of a point,
and put the tiny bits together in a different order, alternating con-
vex and concave, you'd get a straight line exactly the same length
as the circumference. This is just an example of what they might
have said about the difference (or similarity) between points and
lines. No matter how many million little arcs you cut your circumference into, each of them is still a line, with a notional tiny
point at either end. A point, they said, according to Berkeley, was
not quite something, though something more than nothing. But,
Berkeley added, "We Irish think something and nothing next
neighbours."

But what has this got to do with the price of onions? I hear you
enquire. Plenty, I reply. Think of the difference between a one-
legged stool, a two-legged stool, and a three-legged stool on the
one hand, and on the other, a monocycle, a bicycle, and a tricycle.

One-legged stool? Yes indeed, a stout short stick, with a sad-
dle-shaped seat, fitted with a belt, fastened to the top, like the
cross-piece at the top of a T. The belt fastens the stool to the waist
of a farm-hand or dairymaid, and the shaft of the seat protrudes
obscenely from his or her bottom. And—here is the utility making little of any possible obscenity—with hands left entirely free
of possible contaminations the wearer of this stool can move
around from cow to cow at milking time and sit down wherever
there is solid ground to support it. (A two-legged stool, something looking like the figure 11 with a roof, would do the same job
but no better, so why bother?) The tips of the legs of the three-
legged stool form a plane, and so can find a firm level on any surface. A four-legged stool would sit steady only on a surface in the
same plane as the tips of the four legs.

We had just reached her front door as I came to this part of the explanation. "You're a gas man," she remarked with an indulgent grin, "My brother said you're an awful swot but what's all that got to do with bicycles?"

"Well," I began.

"Sorry," she said, "I've got to go in to my tea, but tell me again, won't you? I really mean it, and I'll be off from school early tomorrow because I don't do domestic. And thanks again for tightening the head."

And with that she was gone indoors.

Is it about a bicycle?

As I scorched home, my bike seemed to have some new power of multiplying energy and also a new freedom of movement in all its shafts and bearings. They whirred under me as I pedalled or free-wheeled, quivering with an all-over sense of mingled joy and disappointment: joy at having been given an invitation to call again to go out with this lovely girl; disappointment and annoyance at my own stupid performance, boring a vivacious companion with a personal theory about the universality of three-dom. 'Shouting out the battle-cry of three-dom' in fact. When I called next afternoon, however, she paid me the compliment of asking what the connection was between bicycles and all that stuff about triangles.

"Well," I said, "briefly, a tricycle is theoretically a more efficient piece of apparatus than a bicycle, for the same reasons of stability that make a three-legged stool the best. It establishes its own plane, and it won't fall over when you stop."

"That's all jolly fine in theory," she responded, "but in practice a tricycle has to be much more expensive than a bicycle, and I'm not talking about kids' toy things now, big jobs, with three big wheels and some kind of differential between the rear two to stop falling over at corners and it's got to be heavier to push, think about hills, and my God how are you going to park more than one? You should see our side passage. C'mon, have a look."

She took my hand and led me through the hall to the kitchen

where I again suffered that mixed feeling, the intense pleasure at the touch of her hand and the typical teenage trepidation at being introduced to her mother, who smiled tolerantly as we passed through.

True enough, the side passage was jammed, though only three bikes were parked there and the space available would certainly not house more than one full-grown tricycle. As we dislodged her bike from the other two and edged our way towards the side door, our bodies touched tinglingly for a moment.

"There's another entrance, too," she said, "at the end of the garden; there, giving onto the lane, but we never use it. Some of the neighbours have cars laid up in their garages for the duration, and the odd time they run a car into the lane just to keep it alive, I suppose they hoarded a few gallons of petrol."

But there were no cars on the road to interrupt our pleasant hour's fun, as we put the theory to the test, seeing how slow we could cycle without falling. My imagination flashed a momentary image of the girl and her bike as one, the butterfly handlebars fused into her hands and elbows, her feet in rhythm with the pedals, pumping below the two down-sloping bars of the frame— legs—typical of a girl's bike of the time, flashing below the skirt of her school frock, the saddle and spring carrier hiding metal privacies. I dismissed the vision quickly and guiltily in favour of contemplating the reality.

No need to go on with this. Her brother and I were classmates, as noted. She and my sister were schoolmates, but in classes a year apart. Another friend might have had a sister at the convent but be himself at a third school—we were a loose confederation of companions, some of whom gradually coalesced, coagulated into couples.

SORROWFUL
Third degree

If, as I have suggested, neither Hitler nor Churchill had ever heard of Rathmines, there was nevertheless tangible evidence there of their confrontation. There were little paper flags on pins stuck by my elder brothers into a map of Europe, hanging on the wall of our dining-room, but the war was a distant event happening to other people in other places. Ireland was neutral but a shadowy and fractured IRA courted German help in its perpetual war against Britain. Our road, Belgrave Road, was a hotbed of republicans and radicals. Dr. Kathleen Lynn, our family doctor, a veteran of the war of independence, was very left-leaning in domestic politics, but anomalously, being anti-British, was pro-German. Prof. Johnston across the road from her was an advanced liberal. Her next-door neighbour, my uncle, Frank Dowling, had played Cuchulainn in Pearse's St. Enda's School pageant; he and his wife Sighle Bowen were among the more socialist, his wife was interned by the Free State during the civil war, and had visited the Soviet Union in its early heady days. R.M. Fox, labour historian, was a next-door neighbour of my grandfather, an old IRB man. No surprise then that it was from a house in nearby Castlewood Avenue that a manacled IRA officer escaped and made his way, trailing his clanking chains, to the Garda station in Rathmines. It was Stephen Hayes, who had been imprisoned and tortured by a rival republican faction, who forced from him a 'confession' of double dealing, circulated from a clandestine press.

The more socially conscious republicans were pro-Soviet, and therefore anti-German; the traditional any-enemy-of-England-is-a-friend-of-mine republicans were anti-British and therefore pro-German.

For several hours, one thrilling afternoon, one half of our road was cordoned off by police, no entry or exit permitted, and no word or hint given as to cause or objective. And then Detective O'Brien was shot dead outside his suburban home.

"We had a terrible day in school today," Fionnghuala said, "there's two sisters, the daughters of that detective that was shot. They weren't in school, of course, but the headmistress and the Reverend Mother called us all together first thing and gave us a very severe talking-to about how we should address the two girls when they come back and then we had a Mass for them in the little chapel."

We cycled out to where they lived, it was a big house with a grange gate, a gateway in a cut-stone semi-circular set back from the road, so that carriages could turn, is what we always believed. It was not far from the house with the strange ground-plan, some said shaped like a swastika, in which one of the hapless German spies had been arrested. Even an innocent like me, who had never owned anything in his life, knew that it would have been hard to meet the cost of such homes as the German spy-house or the detached house in its own grounds at the gate of which O'Brien had been shot. Where did a detective sergeant get the money and why was he killed? Rumours abounded, of spies and secret agents, and double agents and *agents provocateurs*, of secret service money diverted from informers to private pockets.

There was more of a police presence in our area, for a while, after these commotions; and I had to make my way home, long after lighting-up time, by a secret route of back lanes, especially useful for a cyclist with no lamp.

Then came the day that she and I spent on our bikes, of course, on a slightly longer trip than usual, to outer suburbs; and, on a rough by-road, near a rushing waterfall, her rear wheel was punctured. We had no repair outfit with us and perforce had to abandon the bike, hiding it in the hedge around a road-side field, for later collection, and giving her a lift home on my cross-bar. (The male bike consisted basically of two triangles of steel tubing, the front triangle outlined from head to saddle to bottom bracket; the rearward from saddle to bottom bracket to rear hub. Not all modern bikes have that convenient upper member, head to saddle, which was the crossbar.) Male chauvinist pig that I was, I enjoyed, intellectually as well as sensually, the nearness of my cross-bar passenger, her hair blowing against my face as we free-wheeled at speed downhill, her shoulders all the time leaning back on my manly chest. A second person on a bicycle not built for two was deemed to be as dangerous to the public as riding a bike without a lamp after dark—and needless to say, our progress after the puncture was slow—so we were doubly incriminated when the dark blue figure stepped from the footpath and waved an imperious hand at us, clearly a signal that we should stop, then and there. To my surprise, there was embarrassment on all sides—he was a neighbour of Fionnghuala's family, knew them all well, in particular her father, a pillar of respectability. He listened to my story of why I was thus offending by two, nodded with a gruff dismissal, and no summons was to follow.

The following day we returned to repair and retrieve her bike. I earned good points for having tyre-levers, a pump, and, especially, the scarce and hoarded rubber solution, a few patches, and a piece of talc, to be grated around repair, the instructions on the tin said, to prevent adhesion to cover (by cover they meant tyre). But I lost points by having to dismount barely beyond the bottom of the first of the slight hills on our way; her slim, trim form on the cross-bar, added to my own bulk and the heavy machine we were riding, proved too much for me. The bonus by-product of course was that walking gave us more time together. This togetherness of two was rudely shattered, however, by the presence of a third, a policeman, leaning on his bicycle, at the gate of what we, for the moment, considered 'our' field. After all, we had got some use for it, no cow or sheep grazed the rough grass, tussocked with rank rushes. We stopped by the gate, expecting some remark from him, and were not disappointed.

"And what is your business here, might I ask?" he enquired ponderously.

"We came to collect a bicycle," I replied, "we had to leave it here yesterday."

"Oh, so you are responsible for that machine, then," he continued, "I suppose you know it's on private property, the landowner noticed it and became suspicious and got in touch with us. And what is your name?" I gave it and he turned his head slightly. "And this young lady?" he enquired. She too gave her name and I heard the 'Fionnghuala' roll musically off her tongue. "I take it the landowner will not wish to incur the expense of taking any action for trespass but that's a civil matter and is no concern of mine. You may have left yourself open to prosecution for wasting the time of the Garda Síochána but these are difficult times and

I'll say no more about that. However, did you know that carrying a person on the cross-bar of a bicycle designed for the carriage of one person has been deemed by the courts to be dangerous driving and to show a lack of due care and concern for other road users, and that offenders may be prosecuted under the Road Traffic Acts?"

With that he leaned down to check that the cuffs of his navy-blue trousers were safely stowed within the tops of his socks, and he strode off, wheeling beside him his heavy iron bicycle by Pierce of Wexford.

Teora póg [old pl. of *trí, ... do thoirbhir t. póga dó*,
she bestowed three kisses upon him ... *Ir.-Eng. Dict.*]

"Crusty oul' divil," I remarked, and set about the repair. The levers gently prised up a short length of the flat tyre's wire-reinforced edge and lifted it over the wheel rim. The rest of that side of the tyre was persuaded over the rim by strong fingers and the flaccid tube was withdrawn. I attached the pump to the exposed valve and with a few quick jets swelled the tube and exerted enough pressure on it internally to cause a slight hiss of air escaping through the puncture. This I found by placing my face close to the tube, and when I felt the little cold spot on my cheek, a delicate tip-of-the-tongue lick applied moisture enough for escaping air to raise a tell-tale bubble and I was able to mark the tiny black hole. A quick rub with the perforated tin grater in the repair kit cleaned the area round the guilty spot, and a few drops of the precious rubber solution were applied to the cleaned area and to one of the equally precious patches. Smeared about, these quickly became tacky to the touch and the patch was as quickly applied to the tube and thumb-held in place. A count of ten, slowly, was enough. Thumb released, and an inspection showed some extrusion of the solution around the edges of the patch. Scraped on the perforated tin grater, the stick of talc yielded a fine powder, which was sprinkled around the repair, as recommended, to prevent adhesion to cover. The tube was fingered back over the rim and under the tyre; the tyre in its turn levered again into place over the rim. I checked carefully that the tube was properly home, and not pinched dangerously between the covered wire edge of the tyre and the metal rim of the wheel. Finally, I pumped the tyre to operational hardness, finger-tightened the valve and stood up.

"Gosh, thanks," Fionnghuala exclaimed, put her arms quickly around my shoulders and as quickly kissed me three times on the lips, "that was great."

GLORIOUS

Why did I volunteer to kill the kittens?

IN THE CITY of Melbourne, Australia, of all places, about two thousand and six, A.D., I saw a group of school-girls moving, almost crocodile fashion, around a wide, pedestrianised plaza, costumed as if for a piece of street theatre, a nostalgia pageant of the 1930s. But I was wrong, the grey felt hats, the red blazers, the white blouses and neck-ties striped blue red and white were all for real. The school principal, I decided, must have designed that uniform with back numbers of the *Girl's Own Weekly* at her elbow. And I compared her product most unfavourably with my vivid memory of the girl I saw in those same thirties. No, I misspeak again, God forgive me for borrowing such a dirty word. The thirties ended with Europe in flames, and Ireland isolated. The war was on, over there; here at home, shortages, rationing, limitations on public transport, lighting—all made for a glorious levelling. And when it was over, many things just picked up where they were in 1939. But it must have been the mid-forties, I realise now, for reasons which will appear.

There were just three of us in that small suburban garden, enjoying late August sun. And I mean small: a garden just about the same size as the footprint, as they say nowadays, of the small, 3-bed semi. There was an even smaller patch at the front, barely enough space for a few dusty bluebells in spring, through it a short path from the gate in the meagre iron railings to the front door. The path was in red tiles, fimbriated in blue. The house was called Oakdene and that incongruous name was set in coloured glass in the fanlight above the front door. Its semi-twin was called The Haven, similarly inscribed in coloured glass, but nobody used these names, the houses were Smiths' or Ryans' or Hugheses'.

Just the three of us: Myrtle, her mother and me. Myrtle and I were squatting on the grass, knees up, hands clasped around the shins, as we chatted about our friends, gossiped about neighbours, wondered would we go to the hop in the tennis club next Saturday, and could we afford it. Myrtle was still wearing her navy blue school frock, knee length, belted or waisted, I don't remember which, but her narrow waist and the wide white collar edged with simple lace together emphasised her burgeoning bosom. She had taken off the long black stockings, and was barefoot. The costume was probably designed to be drab, long-wearing and neutralising, but it was unbearably attractive. No felt helmet here, then, nothing to make her look like a recruit to the Salvation Army; Myrtle's fair hair tumbled curling to her shoulders, and framed that dimpled, smiling face.

Her mother dozed and read, read and dozed, in a deck-chair about a couple of yards from us. If she had been any farther away she would have been over the wall in the next garden. It was from that direction that a sudden distraction came, the large barking of an alarmed dog, the alarmed bark spiced with a high-frequency tinge of doggie panic. There followed a scraping and hissing, as a moth-eaten tomcat scurried up the wall on the far side, stood on the top and glared, his back arched, at the barking dog, then, with a shake of his whole body, leaped nimbly down on our side. Myrtle's mother was awakened by the commotion.

"Oh it's that blasted grey tomcat!" she exclaimed. "He's enough trouble during the day, but you should hear him at night, positively screaming."

"That's not him," Myrtle interposed, "that's the females expressing their delight at his attentions."

This was daring stuff from a seventeen-year-old girl in mixed middle-class company in those days. And her mother surprised me further.

"Yes, well it's a funny way to express delight at that kind of carry-on and you should see the result," she said. "She brought out a litter of kittens yesterday—maybe you've seen them, in the basket just inside the back door there."

As Myrtle and I stood up, her underwear flurried pink.

The kittens looked like a crumpled grey blanket awaiting ironing. A faint and distant whinge filled the air as a ripple altered the shape of the blanket and four or five separate kittens became differentiated. Their queen mother stepped daintily into the basket, curved herself around her progeny, and closed her eyes as they squirmed about, squabbling for access to her nipples.

"Silvery grey seems to be the in colour this season," Myrtle's mother remarked, "both their mammy and their daddy are grey and they obviously take after them. Of course that's if that damn tomcat that haunts our garden is really their daddy—they're a promiscuous lot."

"We can't keep them, that's for sure," Myrtle offered, "what are we going to do about them?" Perhaps a day later, or two, I called again. Myrtle and I were beginning to be spoken of amongst our acquaintances as sweethearts, though the word had a faintly old-fashioned sound. 'Girlfriend' was still slightly American, 'his girl' and 'her fella' were slightly dismissive, 'lovers' of course would have meant that they knew we had consummated our relationship with carnal intercourse. I knew what word I would have liked to use but had never dared speak it even to Myrtle herself. What her mother may have thought of it all was not too clear. We were often left alone together in the front room, and if her mother entered she would apologise as if she had interrupted some intimacy. Apologise! In her own home!

Anyway, it was accepted custom that I might call more or less whenever I liked. Myrtle and I would go cycling together, occasionally calling on various friends and relations with messages from her mother—a telephone in the home then was a mark of the privileged—and in those circles our companionship, I say no more, was taken for granted. On the very rare occasions when we might go to the pictures, Myrtle was expected home by eleven o'clock, as if some moral law depended on the hour of the day. For once she was home the rest of the family might retire for the night and leave us in sole possession of the living room.

Anyway, again to continue the series of events, if that's what a story is, a couple of days after the incident of the dog and the tomcat, I called along and found Myrtle's mother in some distress. "What's up?" I asked, and if I had been asked to classify replies, I got the one I would have described as 'least expected.'

"It's the cats," she said, "Gerry shot the cat but he shot the wrong one."

Gerry was Myrtle's brother, a few years older; old enough to have made a decision for himself to join the British army. Which indeed he did, serving through the D-Day beaches and Market Garden and some time in Germany, and now had just come home on leave—or deserted, or time expired; I didn't ask but this is how I know it all happened in 1945. Though I did ask how come he shot a cat? Myrtle and her mother and I were by now sitting at the kitchen table and Myrtle explained that as a surprise for his parents, he had produced a flat hand-gun in polished steel from his baggage and by way of a good deed had shot the grey cat when his mother the previous evening complained of the sexy screeching. But all cats are grey at night and Gerry's Luger had killed the mother of that silver-grey litter. Alerted to his error by his mother's distress, he had offered to kill the other parent too, if he could find him. This well-meant if naive offer was declined with outrage.

"That one bang is enough to bring the Guards on us," his mother expostulated, "haven't you caused enough trouble? And who's going to feed the kittens now that their mother is gone, and where and why did you get the damn gun anyway?" "I took it off a German officer when he surrendered," he explained, "and I took my water-bottle out of its casing so that I could cut a hole in the bottom to shove the gun in; I thought you and Da might be interested in seeing a trophy. I didn't know until I took it out last night that it had a clip of live ammo in the magazine, it slips up into the butt, and when you started complaining about the caterwauling I thought you'd be glad to be rid of the animal."

Rueful and disappointed, he slammed out the door as he left the house in a huff.

"Where are the kittens?" I asked, "do you want to get rid of them?"

"We'll have to, won't we? We certainly can't afford milk for five hungry infants and I'm not sure where they are, their unfortunate mother was a bit scatty at the best of times and took offence at something or other and carried them off out into the garden in her mouth one after the other. They must be out there somewhere."

Myrtle and I went into the garden and scouted around under the few bushes until we found the sorry little heap of kittens.

"Can you get me a shovel?" I asked Myrtle.

"What are you going to do?" she asked.

"Never mind, it'd be a help if you could get a shovel."

Was it bravado? Was I trying to impress her mother, or discharge some indebtedness to her? Or perhaps to show Myrtle that anything her brother Gerry could do, I could do better? I don't know, but I know it cost me dearly.

I knew what I had to do as she went away to hunt up a garden implement. I had seen an elderly aunt of mine, down the country, kill chickens. A victim under her left arm was clamped firmly between her elbow and her hip, there was a firm grasp of its wings and chest with the left hand, and a quick jerk and twist of the head and neck with the right hand fatally fractured the spine and spinal cord. I was pretty sure the same procedure would work here. I took up one of the kittens and hoped to have the job done before Myrtle came back. But though only three or four days old the kittens were, to my horror, extremely tough. Myrtle was back while I still struggled, twisting and heaving at the tiny animal's neck as it gurgled and whined and emptied its little bowel on my left sleeve. There was nothing for it but to continue the slaughter of the innocents as well as I might, while Myrtle watched with increasing revulsion.

Eventually, I took the shovel from her and dug a hole beside the bush and buried the bodies. She took the shovel back from me silently and I went to the kitchen and washed my hands at the sink, soaping them heavily, and wiped my sleeve as well as I could. Her mother thanked me, in a very small voice.

I visited again a few more times, but Myrtle was always too busy to come out cycling or to chat in the front room and we never went to the hop in the tennis club again. As to what our relationship had been before I slaughtered the kittens, I feel sure her mother knew all the time.

Dot-and-carry-on

DOT No. 1

WE PROTESTED when the crypto-Brits brought out their Union Jacks in College Green on VE night. A trio of hardy souls even made their way into the hallowed halls of Trinity College, mounted narrow stairways to attics and skylights, and with due ceremony tore down the Union Jack which Johnny-come-lately west Brits had flown from the flagstaff on the roof above the entrance. The crowd milling in the open plaza below was a mix of cheerers and booers, some booing the defacement of the flag of Allied victory, others cheering the mounting of the Irish tricolour which replaced it. Later, cocky students from the rival college burnt that Union Jack in the street and some pinned rags of it to their shoes so that they could trample on it with every step.

My name is Rory, an English version of an Irish version of my full given names, Roger Casement, of which I was proud and which I always thought might prove a common bond with Germans, if I should ever meet them. My brothers' given names were Patrick Sarsfield and Owen Roe.

DOT No. 2

We were part of the high-density population of a comfortable middle-class suburb on the south side of Dublin. Tall terraced houses were still occupied by large families, like us, and there was a higher than average concentration on our road of nationalist radicals: a woman who had been medical officer of the Irish Citizen Army in 1916 (and was founder of a Children's Hospital) shared a house with the widow of a pacifist and socialist murdered in 1916 by a deranged British officer; my uncle Frank Dowling, who fought on the republican side in the civil war (as did his wife who did time in gaol for her part in that civil war); a professor of Trinity College, who was a well-known left-wing intellectual; and my grandfather, who was old enough to have been a Fenian before 1916 was dreamt of.

My mother paid a small rent to the Plunketts, a wealthy nationalist family—Killeen Road nearby was named for one of their titles—and a son of that family had been executed after the Easter week rising.

DOT No. 3

I remember seeing my mother crying as I was carried on a stretcher to the motor ambulance (such terms still survived) which was to take me to the Fever Hospital in Cork Street. She knew better than I the dangers I was facing from the fever I had contracted.

After the rash of scarlet fever has subsided ... the skin begins to peel ... and takes about a fortnight thus to shed. This new skin is delicate ... if the patient ... receives a chill ... functions which ought to be carried out by the skin are ... to be performed by the kidneys ... hence follows acute inflammation of these organs, and death after that is often rapid. Nephritis, somebody said, a term no longer appearing in the popular medical encyclopaedias. For treatment, ... *the body should be sponged with cold vinegar and water ... powders and mixtures, as for measles, administered ...* [and] *hot-bran poultice round the throat.* And when all that has been gone through and *when the sick room is vacated, it is not a needless expense to whitewash and repaper it, and the woodwork ought to be thoroughly washed with a solution of chloride of lime, of the strength of 1 lb. to 8 gallons of water.*

I write all this from an old book, as I have no memory of my first days in the hospital; I must have been in some sort of coma. I became aware of messages from home only after what they told me was an interval of several days. My brother cycled to Cork Street with some clothes. He was not allowed to see or speak to me, not allowed beyond the entrance, and the garments he left for me would never go home again but would, after being worn, be thrown in a furnace, incinerated to a charred black nothingness.

We had no telephone in our home but there was a means whereby they might learn some news of me. I was allotted a num-

ber, 1017—it wasn't tattooed on me—and each day they could
consult a table of numbers published in the popular press. 'Progress satisfactory' was the first heading, and it told that all patients
in certain satellite hospitals were doing fine, as were numbers so
and so ... They soon learned that looking there was over-optimis-
tic. They drifted down through a 'Some improvement' table, then
to a block ominously headed 'Condition Unchanged,' and with a
snatch of breath saw me, '1017,' there in the bottom panel among
those headed 'Not so well.'

'1017' gradually worked his way up category by category and
eventually I was sent home, very thin and pale, still fragile but re-
stored to health. I went for the first time to the island, a trip to aid
my recuperation and incidentally to help me in learning the Irish
language, the everyday speech of the islanders. It was there I met
the German.

DOT No.4

It took many hours for the train to cross the country from Dublin to the western city. Bad coal and little of it was the excuse, and
certainly the coal-gas smell pervading the whole set was bad
enough, intimately connected, it seemed, with the snorting puffs
of the engine and its belching of black smoke, its voiding of hissing white steam at intermediate stops. Newspapers were thin,
sometimes down to four pages, even with sensational news, and I
had soon finished reading what accounts there were of the continuing battles behind the Normandy beaches.

A small boy opposite me was armed with a drawing book and
stared helpless at the page open before him. It was sprinkled with
little numbers and the task for the child was to find no. 1 and,
starting from the point so numbered, to draw a line with his pencil to point no. 2, thence to point no. 3, and so continue, until a
picture would be revealed. The boy had clearly never experienced
the revelations of dot-and-carry-on.

"Here," I said, "I'll show you."

I took a pencil from my pocket and laid the book open at the
puzzle page, on my lap, with the bottom of the page towards the

boy. I joined dot no. 1 to dot no. 2 and handed him the pencil.

"Look," I said, "we'll be drawing a picture, can you see the next dot?"

The young woman sitting beside him, presumably his mother, gave me an appreciative smile, but shook her head slightly and dismissively, intimating that the lad was too young, he was not skilled enough with his numbers to turn the scrambled figures, as they seemed, into a picture. After a quick glance at the woman he looked me in the eye, gave me back the pencil and whispered, "You do it."

Childish, if you like, but done slowly it would fill a quarter of one of the hours on a journey which threatened to be very long. The jerky line, awkwardly twisting, finally turned itself into a picture of a ship with a single funnel, flying an indeterminate flag at its stern.

*

The real ship was a small general-purpose craft, 130 feet stem to stern, and beamy, at 36 feet (I looked it up in another book), built in 1912 for the Congested Districts Board. She was to ferry goods and passengers among the islands off the west coast and the barren patches and pockets on the mainland, where people so outstripped potatoes that the townlands were deemed 'congested.' If brass and mahogany lent her finish the faded Edwardian look of her distant youth, the massive protrusion of her stern over the screw below was like an early Victorian bustle. The skirt, her low-slung rails amidships, was broken here and there with removable gates.

Through an open hatch I watched the triple pistons working in the engine-room below, their steam-driven pushes on the shaft burning up to five tons of coal on the trip from the mainland to the island and back.

When we reached the island, the purpose of those gaps in the rails became clear. There was no dock or jetty and we lay to at anchor off-shore. We were joined there by a small fleet of currachs.

A few of these twenty-foot rowboats of lath and tarred canvas trailed bullocks behind them, wide-eyed and roaring. These were destined for the jobbers who would pass them on to be fattened in the midlands — that is, if they could survive the terror of being forced to swim from shore with nooses round their necks, then being plucked from the sea by slings slipped under their bellies, hoisted onboard by a line to the sheerlegs and down to a pen in the open hold.

Currachs with less troublesome charges formed a tidy queue in line abreast alongside, first-come catching ropes' ends near one of those gateways in the rail, next in the line holding station by gripping the gunwale of the preceding, and so on. Each in turn did its business with the ship, collecting sacks of flour or cement, barrels of stout, delivering men and women in unaccustomed city clothes, passengers for the steamer to take back to the mainland city for medical attention, to visit relatives, for major shopping. And then passed the holding ropes to its next neighbour and pulled away.

An Atlantic swell bore the currachs up and down and an anxious young mother waited her turn to go down the narrow iron ladder on the ship's side and clamber into the heaving boat; but first she had to secure the passage of her precious infant, born on the mainland no more than a couple of weeks before, by fearfully dropping it into the waiting arms of its proud father, as ship and currach rose and dipped synchronously on the undulating sea.

Eighty or one hundred yards away, the swell lapped on a curved beach and squealing teenage girls, home from mainland school, were carried the last few yards, from currach to shore, by strong young men wading, whose wet feet and trousers were a small price for the moments of playful public intimacy. Most of these men were wearing blue-grey homespun, tailored roughly into sleeved waistcoats, and baggy trousers held at the waist by woven woollen girdles.

She was sitting in the third currach in the queue, smiling at the steamer's day-tripper passengers, crowded along the rails of the main and boat decks.

DOT No. 6

She sat in the currach, perfectly at ease, a smile on her round face, the firm flesh over her high cheekbones crinkled under her grey eyes by that smile, the whole framed with her shining dark, almost black, curling hair. She was wearing a wide and long skirt of deep maroon, so long I could not see her feet. She might have been barefoot, or she might have been wearing the local raw cowhide slippers, as were several of the men in the boat with her. There was a multicoloured woven square shawl over her shoulders, orange and blue, green and red, and black and white, folded into a triangle, points crossing on her breast and tucked into the top of her skirt, the other corners draped elegantly down her back.

"There's Brighdín," I muttered urgently to my brother, then aloud called "Brighdín, Brighdín!"

She heard and scanned the row of passengers lining the rail and staring in fascination at the lateral queue of currachs. For a long moment she recognised noone, then at last, as her boat finished its business and drew away, she ejaculated my name, "Rory!"

I wondered how she would negotiate those last yards to the beach, would some young man be lucky enough to carry her in his arms, or, barefoot, would she lift that skirt over her knees and paddle through the susurrating surf as it lapped, fondling, around her ankles?

DOT No. 7

I had a folding camera. Its pleated bellows had to be slid forward on tiny steel runners when the front flap of the apparatus was folded open and down. I was a rotten photographer, I know it now, like most bad workmen blaming my tools. The fuzzy black and white images showed greyish figures—"That's Brighdín on the coral strand," I would have to explain—with flaring sunlight behind them; behind them, for God's sake. The camera had three shutter speeds, none fast enough to immobilise in a picture the rolling and crashing waters of the Atlantic as they burst on the island's iron-bound shore. But I had to try it, and did it so close to the incoming combers that I backed away startled as I clicked the shutter. The waters in foam and the immemorial rocks were all shaken and soft-edged in the print and the whole thing looked like a display of dirty cotton wool.

DOT No. 8

The scattered population of the island was no more than a couple of hundred, in low density throughout a few clusters of cottages hardly deserving the name of villages. Only one of them had a 'shop,' a pub which never seemed to run out of stout but whose supplies of bread, flour and other domestic staples never lasted more than a few days after re-supply by the visiting steamer.

Basically, the house was your typical Irish country cottage; thatched, three rooms long, entrance door (plus half-door) giving on the main room or kitchen in the middle. Three other doors from that kitchen, one to each of the other rooms, at either end of the cottage, and one, nearly opposite the entrance door, which led to a small yard. There were two lofts, floored spaces under the roof and over the two end rooms. The kitchen itself was not ceilinged, but a gesture had been made towards whitewashing the inside of the roof's thatch, stained by the smoke from the turf fire smouldering constantly in the open hearth, with hooks above it from the swinging arm of a soot-blackened crane. The heady, tangy scent of the burning turf caught my breath and effectively emancipated me all of a sudden from the bourgeois manners and customs of Belgrave Road, Rathmines.

So basically, yes, your typical country cottage, but the house had been altered. An unskilled hand had run up a lean-to of corrugated iron with tarred felt roof in the yard, to accommodate members of the family when they withdrew annually from the main building to leave rooms for summer visitors. That time, the summer visitors were the German, snugly occupying the larger of the two lofts, and me, allotted the smaller of the rooms off the kitchen.

DOT No. 9

I was not a total stranger to country life, with minimum facilities, no running water — carry it by the bucket from a well or spout — and only candles and an oil-burning lamp for artificial lighting, with the lamp used but sparingly as the oil was scarce and the wicks and chimneys were hard to replace. And cooking on an open fire. And a dry closet for the lavatory. All these I knew from summer camps with Fianna Éireann, the patriotic republican Boy Scouts' organisation.

We wore green tunics with brass buttons, and white lanyards for our signalling whistles, and felt hats like the Royal Canadian Mounted Police, but green. My brother played martial airs on the bagpipes for the troop's close-order foot-drill: 'Let Erin Remember,' 'Wrap the Green Flag,' 'Who Fears to Speak,' 'O'Donnell Abú,' 'Kelly, the Boy from Killaan,' 'Step Together,' 'Viva la,' 'A Nation Once Again,' 'Deep in Canadian Woods,' 'God Save Ireland,' 'The Boys of Wexford,' 'The Legion of the Rearguard.'

Each summer we spent a week at camp on Kilmashogue in the hills south of Dublin. We were taught to perform the household tasks quickly each morning — prepare the food, eat it, tidy up, wash up, get the next meal ready, tend to fire and fuel supply — then off out to the mountainside for the day's 'games.' Mr. Plunkett, the Leader, had us divided into teams. We were taught to spread out in a long line, hiding as best we could among the heather bushes, as we crawled, only one boy moving at a time, trying to approach and surprise the competing team. More simply described, it could have been called a skirmishing order manoeuvre in platoon strength.

When tall men in long overcoats got out of a car at the bottom of the lane leading to our campsite, Mr. Plunkett quickly called an end to that game and instead set us chasing and capturing one another, just like school yard relievio.

In the evening round the campfire we were given exciting talks and illustrated leaflets about heroes of the patriotic past — the rescue of the Fenian prisoners from western Australia, Owen Roe's victory at Benburb, the escape of the Ulster princes from Dublin Castle under Queen Elizabeth.

DOT No. 10

The first thing I noticed was the word 'Heidelberg' in big red letters across the front of his white sweater, clothing a hefty torso. He gave me a smiling welcome, speaking in Irish, correct and only slightly accented. I replied equally fluently but with the even less traditional accent of my Dublin school Irish and we quickly established that his English was better than my Irish. My German was limited to stock phrases and the words of a few songs, so English it was to be.

"Heidelberg," I said, gesturing towards his jersey, "there aren't many from there on holidays hereabouts at this stage of the world's history. I suppose you know the British and Americans have landed in Normandy?"

I offered the thin newspaper.

"Thanks, I heard," he replied, "but I'm not on holidays."

"How come?"

"I came to Ireland in 1939 and the war broke out and I couldn't get home." Then, a little sniffily, "I work all winter teaching German and giving a few music performances and I've been spending the summers here ever since, they know me well."

(I should point out that I do not have total recall of every conversation I had with him, especially those which took place in the pub, but I am surer of my recollection of the facts he passed on to me about himself and am doing the best I can at reconstructing our chats. And by the way he had never heard of Roger Casement.)

"Not meaning to pry," I asked once, " but I've wondered what brought you here in the first place?"

"I was in a group of post-graduates in *Anglistik* — that includes Irish studies and I know that annoys Irish people — and there was a scholarship for one of us to come to Ireland for a couple of months to study the Celtic race, ethnography, folklore, language, anthropometrics, the lot."

"Weren't you lucky to win that scholarship, and what in the name of God is anthropometrics?"

"Lucky? I didn't win it, it wasn't given as a prize, the award was made by the University, to a student who was an enthusiastic Nazi party member, but he got ill, and at the last minute they had to find somebody else, and I fitted the part. Anthropometrics involves measuring peoples' heads and bodily dimensions, it was all the rage, but I did very little of that, the people here wouldn't wear it." "How do you mean, fitted the part?" "Tall and blonde,"— he passed his fingers through his hair, glinting gold-to-reddish in the sun—"the right shape if you like, that's what you have to be to get on in the thousand-year *Reich*, and my father was in the Free Corps after the first war, fighting against the communists in Bavaria; he thinks Hitler is marvellous."

"What about yourself?"

"Oh I'm a member of the *Hitlerjugend* all right, unless I've become disqualified by being over-age now—we all had to be members and it was great for the hiking and the camping and the sing-songs."

Very conscious that Ireland was neutral, I nevertheless wanted to show that some of us at least were not unfriendly toward the enemies of our traditional enemies.

"How about your comrades, then?" I asked, "did they all finish up in the army? They had some wonderful victories."

"For all I know, they're all frozen to death in the heart of Russia, we were supposed to be gaining living space there but we've only got dying space."

And tersely: "I have no news from home."

DOT No. 11

I was back on the island a year or so later and the German was gone. In the interval I had seen two sets of searing images which changed my life for all time. And they were so similar. Cavernous, hollowed faces, sunken cheeks and sunken staring eyes, tattered garments hanging on gaunt bodies hunched against the cold, against the world, against death. But in the one case, they were in striped overalls and prostrate on the narrow wooden shelves of crowded barracks, with numbers tattooed on their wrists; survivors in Auschwitz, Bergen-Belsen, Buchenwald, Neuengamme, Ravensbruck, barely rescued in time from being thrown in a furnace and incinerated to a charred black nothingness. In the other, they were the survivors of a whole German army, ground into the dirt in the ruins of Stalingrad, squatting in the snow, skin peeling from frost-bite (*the new skin is delicate ... if the patient receives a chill ... death after that is often rapid ...*). Or shuffling to the horizon in lines of endless thousands, defeated by the *Untermenschen* of the east, and prisoners now of the victorious and vengeful Russians.

DOT No. 12

Our Holocaust denial had a short half-life, and its half-hearted reasons quickly evaporated—the dead had died of typhus, an epidemic brought about when the disruptions of the final battles destroyed all the services to the camps for displaced persons, so it was really the fault of the Americans and their bombing. And the furnaces too were for the control of contagion, to burn up infected garments. And all those thousands of survivors made tattoos of numbers on their own wrists, with the bureaucratic back-up which ensured that the numbers were all different, just for fun, or maybe to continue a systematic denigration of the noble Germanic race? Such bullshit! Oh such bullshit.

DOT No. 13

Brighdín told me what had happened.

"Two tall men in long overcoats came on the steamer one day, they came to the door and asked for him. He just took his rucksack which he had ready and went away with them back to the steamer ... I didn't think he could have taken all his stuff so I went up to his loft and looked around ... his guitar was there with a note in Irish saying I could have it ... then there was a small attaché case I hadn't ever noticed before ... I opened it and there was some sort of wireless in it like the one we hear the football matches on beyond at the pub only smaller and this one had a handle like the handle you turn on my mother's sewing machine or the handle for winding up a gramophone and clipped onto the inside of the lid there was a thick block of tickets like they have for the raffle for the church, only they just had numbers on them, in tables like you'd learn your tables from in school, no other writing … you can't hide anything on this island … if he'd thrown it away everybody would have known where it came from because they'd know it hadn't come from anywhere else and even if he'd thrown it in the sea somebody would have seen him do it or the people out watching for floating wreckage would have found it … they see everything … he hugged and kissed me once, on the way home from the pub one night, and everybody knew, and they all laughed at me and called after me to know how was the anthropometrics …"

DOT No. 14

I saw him once again, in the coincidence which prompts this rambling reminiscence, but my seeing him was of no consequence to anyone but myself, the actual event was public knowledge. It must have been in 1947, I was applying for a passport for the first time; it was beginning to be possible to travel again as the world settled down. I was standing in a queue in the Passport Office, then located in an old building just outside the gate of Dublin Castle. Moving forwards a few steps at a time we were suddenly hustled to one side by policemen. "Out of the way there," "Stand back there," "Stand aside, will you." On a stretcher borne with some difficulty down the narrow stairs there was an inert figure, partly covered with a blanket. The face was flushed an ugly bright purple but it was my German. Threatened with deportation, and fearing (groundlessly) the consequences of what might be discovered about him in his homeland, he had condemned himself to death, had bitten the capsule.

But what charge had he brought against himself, what guilt or shame was he confessing? I shall never know.

Daisy daisy

Two shots from a legally-held shotgun

A BEAUTIFUL GIRL *came in his sleep to Aonghus the god of love,
but as he reached out to touch her she vanished.*

*Night after night she appeared and disappeared until a magician
told him her name and the name of the lake where she was to be
found. The magician warned him that for one half year, from Bealtaine to Samhain, she would be in the form of the beautiful girl he
had seen, then from Samhain to Bealtaine she would be in the form
of a bird. Aonghus went to the lake and saw there a flock of fifty white
swans. As he watched, they put off their white plumage and became
a merry band of girls, linked by a chain of silver. Last to change was
the beautiful girl of his dreams, adorned with a necklace of burnished
gold. As she swam he stole her golden necklace and feathered cloak
and with these in his power he too turned into a swan, cob to her pen,
from Samhain to Bealtaine, and it was as swans they flew round the
great hostel of the fairy folk at Newgrange on the Boyne, Brú na
Bóinne, charming all within with their beautiful music. From Bealtaine to Samhain they lived and loved as man and woman.*

*

I try to pretend to myself that I can keep them all at arm's length,
it has nothing to do with me, they are just old acquaintances, but
it doesn't really hold up. I know the scene it all emerged from so
well—the suburban tennis club, that cottage in a small field on
the canal bank, the village folklore, all burnt into my soul with
the searing clarity of late youth and early manhood.

It must have begun on that gala day of the tennis club. More
of a social club, really, no aspirant to ranking tournaments ever
came from Greenane, even in mixed doubles, which was a popular event there.

On a summer gala day, when the finals of the few little tournaments had been played, the annual club sports was held—all
the old reliables, obstacle race, sack-race, egg-and-spoon race,
three-legged race (what wonderful broad witticisms that evoked),
and the wheel barrow race. Not with real wheel-barrows, of
course, the whole glorious sunlit afternoon was a fun event, one
good laugh after another.

The wheel-barrow race was an event for pairs, or rather couples, barrow and barrow-boy. The barrow-'boys' were girls, as the
role of barrow was deemed too strenuous for any but muscular
males. The barrows lined up at the start lying nearly flat on the
ground, face down, and with their heads pointing towards the
winning tape fifty or sixty yards away. The barrow-boys, standing
behind the barrows, or below their feet, if you like, took hold of
the legs of the barrows and tucked the ankles under their arms, or
otherwise treated those legs like the handles of a barrow. On the
blast of the starting whistle, each barrow raised his head and
shoulders off the ground by straightening his arms and started
forward with 'steps' of his hands, left, right, left, right. These
hands stepping forward made the 'wheel,' as the legs held by the
girls were the handles. Hence wheel-barrow race. The irregular
pulling and lopsided leg-holding by giggling girls led to crossing
of lanes, collisions of wheel-barrow into wheel-barrow, boy into
boy, girls dropping the legs of their partners, and general collaps-
es into storms of merriment.

Was Trish a tomboy? The boys loved her and she shone in
their company, spoke that little bit louder, pushed away those
hands that little bit less energetically, and was a sore loser. If anybody was going to show attitude in the whee-barrow race, it was
bound to be she. And she did it by the simple means of reversing
the usual roles. She grabbed Danny, and not taking 'no' for an answer, spoke sharply, "C'mon, Danny boy, here, grab my legs, we
can win this."

Danny's stronger male arms were holding lighter 'handles'
than the other competitors and Trish's 'wheeling' was enjoying
stronger support—they had all the advantages, and won easily.

And Danny boasted later of his bonus, exclaiming "I could see right up, her skirt was flapping as we ran the race, she had frilly panties on, with no elastic in the legs. Whahoo!" There was an informal dance—a hop—on the evening of the gala day. 'Informal' meant that the tennis gear was still OK and she was still wearing that divided short skirt. Only soft drinks, and no tablets, but blood was young, there was no need for stimulants or epileptic lighting: instead, quicksteps and foxtrots, the odd tango for the experts, slow waltzes for smooching; all gave the chance for a quick hug and surreptitious touching. During the 'excuse me' set, a procession of hopefuls tipped her partners on the elbow—"Excuse me, Jimmy!" or Bill or Johnnie or Alf—all anxious to have a whirl around the pavilion floor with Trish moving easily in their arms. And there was weeping and gnashing of teeth by the disappointed each time the M.C. called out 'ladies' choice' and some lucky guy enjoyed her favour.

It might have been Danny who saw her home after the hop, but whoever it was, if her parents were at home, all he could expect in response to his whispered 'give us a kiss' was another quick hug and perhaps a slightly longer good-night kiss as they stood on the doorstep. The writ of the Redemptorists still ran. One of them, Fr. Duggan, had come and preached at the annual school retreat, hired by local management to introduce teenage boys to what were coyly called the facts of life. This he did in public and in private. In private, in the secrecy of the confessional, he quite coldly and brutally told the pimply penitents that "that organ in the front of your body sometimes gets stiff and some boys might rub it to make it stiffer—and you wouldn't do anything like that? Because it's gravely sinful." In public he stated baldly to the congregation, for this instruction restricted to senior classes only, "A girl's breasts are sexual, and very highly so, and sometimes she experiences a terrific desire to be embraced." As he said this, his hands, lightly cupped, were held to his chest in simulation of the notorious breasts. Any cooperation in indulging this desire of the girls was also—easy to guess it—gravely sinful.

The girls were probably getting the same kind of instruction in their school retreat, but if they did, Trish was not one to pay much attention. Perhaps demonstrating the Duggan proposition, she relaxed briefly against her escort's chest as they embraced and kissed goodnight.

The last event on the club's calendar that year, and what proved to be the last event in the club's history, was the autumn cycle excursion. Cars were only just beginning to come onto the roads again, following the petrol-famine of the Second World War, but we all had bikes—I suppose I should say push-bikes, a term quaint and old-fashioned, but necessary to distinguish our Rudges and Raleighs from the mopeds and motor-bikes which soon followed. And needless to say Trish on this occasion too managed to establish her usual one-up position. She begged or borrowed a tandem and 'volunteered' Danny to be her co-pedallist on this bicycle-made-for-two. Their legs were linked by chains and sprocketed wheels, and pistoned together in exact synchronisation; they quickly left the struggling *peloton* far behind and must have been in the Massey woods a full half-hour or more before the others began arriving at the picnic-site. Knowing nudges and winks— it's the cliché—were exchanged when it was noted that the fire had only just been lit. "Did you have much trouble finding firewood in the woods?" "Was there no kindling around?" "That tandem put a lot of space between you two and the rest of us." "Did you have to go far into the bushes?" "Was it hot enough without any fire?" Masters of subtlety, the boys in our club.

Over the winter, as business picked up, the owner of Greenane found that there was a market for building land and sold his fields. The new owner demolished the corrugated iron pavilion with little more than a push and a shake and, for lack of a venue, the club never re-convened. Anyway, the skinny dipping had made it unpopular in the neighbourhood. In the western suburbs of Dublin, it was quite close to the Grand Canal. The canal's city reaches, boxed in with concrete and tarmac, were cluttered with the battered frames of prams and bikes, but a short step along the tow-path took walkers to pleasant levels of clean smooth water between grassy banks.

August was very warm that year and it seemed natural for the revellers, after that evening dance which ended the club's gala day, to take a romantic moonlit stroll on the waterside.

Two swans swam away, disappearing in the dim light, as we entered the tow-path, two by two. Someone who knew his Yeats or Pádraic Colum or whoever it was, intoned the lines "as the swan in the evening, moved over the lake . . ."

"*Swan Lake?*" a voice rejoined, from someone who knew his ballet, "You girls better look out, it's getting late and at midnight you might be turned into swans by an evil magician."

"Lake?" came a further response in the dark, "Sure it's only a bloody canal."

"Yeah, but, y'know, it's lovely and clean out these parts."

"We've no togs, or we could go for a midnight swim."

"Ah sure it's black dark, nobody'd see us."

"But we've no towels to dry ourselves with."

"Can't we just run up and down the bank, you eejit, and slap ourselves dry."

The noise of splashing was counterpointed with slaps and giggles and it wasn't that dark—it never is. When Trish returned to the tidy little heap where she had left her clothes—bra and singlet, that famous divided skirt and the frilly panties, and her white socks and tennis shoes—the bra and singlet were missing.

A hoarse male whisper: "Hey lads, here's a bit of gas, take hold of this," and a small soft bundle changed hands several times before disappearing.

"Oh you're a right gang of lousers," she said. She demanded Danny's shirt and made her way home with it flapping about and sticking here and there to her wet body. But somebody told somebody and the story grew, in the minds of Clondalkin village, into a debauched Bacchanalian orgy.

*

As former members drifted apart there was only the occasional opportunity to exchange gossip about mutual acquaintances but word did pass around of Trish's crisis—"She'll have to swap the tandem for a pram!"

"God, this is terrible," her father said. Then, turning to her mother, "This is all your bloody fault, bringing the two of us night after night to that bloody bridge club, I knew something like this could happen." And turning back to the sullen girl, "When did it happen? I mean when is it due to happen? And who's responsible?" "June," she said, adding: "Danny." "Do we know him? Does he know about it? What are you going to do about it?" "He's been here, if you paid any notice. He knows. I don't know."

Later, in more collected mood, he asked Danny out straight, "Damn it, lad, do you love the girl?"

The reply was at best non-committal: "Well, I like her."

"For Chrissake, boy, do you like her, as you put it, enough to marry her?"

"I suppose so."

So Mammy and Daddy rustled up a distant cousin in holy orders and Trish and Danny were married very early one winter morning in the chapel-of-ease of a remote suburban parish. It was that temporary chapel of corrugated iron which wandered round the diocese year after year, dismantled and re-erected as the catholic demographics dictated.

Then Daddy's friends in public life arranged a job for Danny on the city pay-roll—not much of a job, but a job—and a house for the young couple on a local authority estate, all in time for the birth in late spring of a little son. She emphasised the 'little' and drew attention to the smallness of his nails, evidence of how premature he was, would you believe.

We visited them a couple of times, at her pressing invitation, conveyed by telephone. Further lobbying of Daddy's influential friends had had a public phone kiosk installed near their front door.

We arrived a little early for an evening meal on one of these visits and Danny followed us into the house, home from work, in clay-streaked overalls. "Your bath is ready," she said, "I've had the fire on for a good while and the water should be hot enough."

Danny failed to take the hint, and sat down to chat for a while, clay-streaked overalls and all.

"Did you have to take two buses from your place?" he asked, "Must be a damn nuisance, one into town from your place then another out to here."

"We'll have the tea on the table in a few minutes," she said, "you better get bathed and changed." He looked at her in some surprise as he rose to act on her suggestion and paused beside the pram where the baby boy was sleeping peacefully.

"Hi, chuggins," he said, or some such mock-word of endearment, and gave the pram a gentle rocking.

"Don't waken the baby," she cautioned, "I'll put on the kettle while you're dressing." We listened to Radio Luxembourg while we ate our sliced ham, lettuce, and bread and butter, followed by cup-cakes.

"Funny, isn't it?" he speculated, "They've never managed to invent a wireless run on gas." We all paused to digest this. "I mean," he continued, "they always try to compete, look at ovens and cookers and grills and toasters and lights and gas-fires and electric fires."

I certainly wasn't going to start then and there explaining about thermionic valves and emission of particles under heat. There was an uncomprehending pause and she broke in with a weak play on words, "Well some of the programmes on the wireless are great gas anyway," and the chat moved on.

When the word was passed around that they had split, nobody was really surprised; they were an ill-assorted pair at the best of times. In an odd sort of way the location of the club at the edge of the city had been the cause of their problems, bringing chaps like Danny from the rural side into contact with people like Trish from the city side. Everybody was sympathetic. They knew that Danny was a bit naïve, unsophisticated; and that the pushy Trish had a well-heeled middle-class background and some education.

We heard of the split-up, of course, only when it was already over, and the question already answered which sprang first to everybody's mind: what about the kid? The kid, happily, was OK, and had been taken by a welcoming but childless aunt and her husband. There was no formal adoption, just as there was no formal divorce or separation; people just did these things.

Trish, the scuttlebutt, ran, had gone to England, and Danny had gone to live alone in the cottage left by his deceased parents, farther out along that same canal. We visited him there, to show solidarity. I had never been in such a house before. "Nice place you have here," I said, glancing around appreciatively.

"It's alright," he replied briefly, as if surprised that anyone should see anything about his little house that was at all remarkable.

It was a three-room cottage, with small windows piercing the thick walls; the central room, in which we sat, was entered directly from the small yard. A large open fireplace occupied most of one of the walls dividing this kitchen, the heart of the house, from the end-rooms. A turf fire smouldered in the deep grate and a large iron kettle, gently sizzling, hung above it from a swinging crane with hooks and chains.

"Cut your own turf?" I asked.

"Yeah, it's not too far away. Like a cup of tea?"

The tea, like everything else, was tinged with the ancient perfume of the smouldering turf.

"I love the smell of the turf fire," I remarked, "you miss it with closed stoves and coal and all in the city."

"Do you have gas fires?" he asked, "I mean there's bottled gas coming in now." And so the aimless talk went on. After the tea, which he served reasonably well, considering, I made a gesture showing that I needed to use the facilities. He grinned and waved an arm towards the open countryside.

"The old pair never got round to it," he explained, "it's one of the things I must do, fix up some kind of a toilet but meantime there's the bushes. Careful where you step."

I did my pee in the bushes and on my return to the kitchen splashed some water from a jug over my hands and into a waste bucket.

Our visits to the canal-side house showed, we hoped, that we sympathised with Danny, without taking sides in any matrimonial dispute. The nearest I ever got to family matters had been an insouciant enquiry of "How's the little lad?" which got the brief response, "Oh he's grand, his aunty's spoiling him rotten." To preserve our neutrality we accepted visits from Trish when, after a lapse of some years, she began to call on her old acquaintances.

"I mean it's very nice where I am, the old lady I help to look after is very nice too, but it's nice to come home"— (home?) — "and hear all your news, just like old times, I mean I thought of you when I was in France there recently and I stopped to look at people playing tennis, boys and girls like in our old club, and anyway there was this man standing there watching them too and his English was very good, I mean my French is terrible, I was never any good at languages at school, except Irish of course, which we had all the time at home, more or less; anyway we chatted away and he asked me to come home with him and he and his wife were terribly nice to me and they had this big house in the country with servants and all and they wanted me to stay longer but I had a flight booked ..." She obviously had something going for her still but would she ever stop talking for an odd second or so? And what was the real story behind this virtual pick-up?

Next time around, or maybe next but one, when we went to visit him in his canal-side cottage, he had acquired a two-seater canoe. Why not? And he living beside calm water; no storms, no waves, just gentle paddling and silent gliding along a placid linear lake. He instructed me in the basics of the craft—weight through your arms on both gunwales, bum in first, spine upright, work the paddles left and right as if rotating round gimbals in front of your chest. A few wobbles and I had it. To make the trip useful we set off for the nearest bridge over the canal, there to leave the water and walk up the road to the village for a refreshing pint.

Paddling past a reed-bed, we disturbed a family of swans. The hefty male puffed out his wide white wings, and drew back his head and neck into the space between. Then, with massive strokes of power, he swam towards us, hissing. I was scared, as every schoolboy knows that a swan can break your arm with a whack of one of those wings.

"Look at those two birds swimming!" I cried, but Danny was used to this, and a few slaps of his paddle on the surface of the water had that angry cob keeping his distance; eventually he turned westward and stroked away. As the pen, his mate, emerged from behind the reed-bed, we drifted gently towards the bank and waited, to allow the whole family of swans to move away together; but she started east, accompanied by a clutch of grey cygnets, frantically paddling to keep up with her.

"Eff that for a lark," Danny exclaimed. "We can't wait all day for them." A few paddle strokes brought us again to midstream; and we were, despite our best efforts, dividing the swan family. We were following the cob, and the pen and cygnets had turned to follow him too, though at a distance, and were now trailing along behind us. In that order we eventually reached the bridge, where we put the canoe on the hard and started to walk to the village.

We were joined by an elderly local man who had watched with some amusement over the parapet of the bridge as the swan and canoe procession approached along the waterway below. He chuckled as he recounted the incident to his mates in the pub.

"There they were, chasing after the proud father and the mammy and the kids chasing after them." Then turning to us, "They mate for life, you know," he explained, "good family people, the swans." He glanced at Danny. "And they're dumb," he added. "I mean dumb like mute, not dumb like stupid, and they only sing when they're dying, did you know that?"

To make some contribution to the conversation, I said, "They look like big geese to me: what's the real difference? They all seem to love the water."

He looked at me with the countryman's pity for the city slicker.

"Sure lookit," he said, "the swan's a big bird, lovely and white, with a big long neck and an orange-coloured bill with a black knob on it. A goose—" he paused, "a goose is no real colour at all, sort of greyish and brownish, only sometimes white, with a short neck and a stubby beak, like a big duck really, and it grazes grass like a cow and shits all over the place and leaves your yard filthy and as slippery as ice."

"We used always have a goose for Christmas," Danny contributed. "Can you eat swan?"

I knew he had a shotgun — I had seen him now and then fire at the crows, jackdaws, magpies and sea-gulls which invaded his small garden as soon as ever his vegetable seedlings showed their defenceless heads above ground — and I knew what way his mind was probably working.

"B'God now, you could try, you could try, but I wouldn't recommend it. They had bad times over the water during the war when they had very little meat and there was a chap here used to net the odd swan and make a few bob selling them to a man in the meat exporting business beyond in the market in Dublin but he never had any good of it in the latter end; he died soon after very young." He paused again, this time for a slug of his pint. "It was nettin' he did, I'm pretty sure." Another pause. "He could 'a been shootin' them, only it was during the war and there was no cartridges to be had." A longer pause. "They're a very special bird, them swans, you wouldn't want to interfere with them."

A phone call heralded another visit from Trish one summer and it's very hard to say 'no' when an old acquaintance says she's coming over, and will we be at home? She'd love to call and see us. She gave the bus's time of arrival but did not mention the size and weight of the case which was the major part of her baggage, though not the whole of it. I was unable to lift it and so had to 'walk' it, tilting and shifting corner after corner on the ground, to the rear seats of our small car.

"In the name of God," I asked, "what on earth have you got in this, lead ingots?"

Ask a stupid question and you get a stupid answer:

"I'm away for three weeks and I only brought five outfits, and I didn't know when I'd be able to do any laundry and there's some things I brought that I won't be bringing back because Jean wanted me to get some things in Birmingham that she said she couldn't get here. She called on me there and we had tea, and I asked her to stay, but she was very grateful and said I'd been very helpful to her already, and she insisted I was to call when I come over, I mean if you can't help people out things have come to a pretty pass, that's what I always say, so I'll be leaving some of the stuff in this case with Jean when I leave her place where I'll only be able to spend a few days ..."

Who is Jean, and where is she? Don't ask, but it was clear that Trish had no intention of moving on farther that day; we had to lodge her and her baggage, not to mention help her to wash her dirty linen.

Danny continued to be concerned, if only slightly, at the lack of facilities in his cottage. His water-supply was carried in a bucket from a nearby well, but the very existence of that well was one of the reasons for care in the disposal of human waste, which might pollute the ground water; and the ground water, despite what diviners say, is everywhere. He had collected leaflets describing a number of installations for disposing of waste and they all managed to avoid any more explicit term. Turd, faeces, excrement, all seem perfectly safe and inoffensive standard English words but they never used them, never mind the vernacular four-letter (five-letter?) version. Sewage, solids, human waste is as close as they got. ('Dung' was the word Danny used when he didn't say 'shit,' but 'dung,' like 'manure' or 'droppings' or 'spraint,' would properly apply only to the animal product; just as humans don't have 'paws,' except jocosely.)

Next step above 'the bushes' was the outhouse with a wooden seat, hole in the middle of the seat over a bucket. This dry closet system still had its advocates, including a professionally qualified horticulturalist who wrote to the *Irish Times* saying that, alas, the dry closet was superseded by the more congenial (nicely put!), but environmentally disastrous WC. But the DC buckets had to be emptied. Ditto the impressive Elsan range, from the Minitoilet (complete with anti-spill lid), to the Bristol, and the Portaflush III (completely hygienic and odourless sanitation). And the Carlew three-stage septic tank (effluent flows into the main tank, where solids settle and are biologically digested). And the BioFilter and the Saniflo ... There was a review in a gardening magazine, where you might expect them to call a spade a spade, of the coyly named 'Humus' toilet (winner of the gold medal at the International Exhibition at Geneva). "All the waste matter," the best they could manage, "is composted down to a nice clean friable state that is completely safe and odour-free and in appearance very similar to turf." It is, in fact, the review tells us, a compost bin with a seat on top. One of the leaflets had as head-piece a travesty of Rodin's *Thinker*, suggestively posed as if seated on a you-know-what. The manufacturer's leaflet for the Humus job tells us that, mercifully, an automatic compost cover connected to the seat gives a simple yet effective visual barrier.

This *Thinker*-headed Humus, then, is a grotesque figure for the Freudian subconscious and its censor, it packages the waste products of existence and dishes them up safe, unfrightening and odour-free, but bland, even boring.

In the long run, what with building restrictions, lack of running water, lack of electricity, high cost, the high water-table, all he could do was bury a slurry tank, wash the turds into it through a pipe with a jug of canal water, and every so often hire a local man with the right machine to pump it out.

Anybody should have realised what had been happening when she said that word as if it meant no more to her than 'cyclists' or 'non-smokers.' Later, in the privacy of our bedroom with our visitor safely out of earshot, I asked my wife who the hell this Thomas was?

"Oh," she told me, rather dismissively, "he's just one of a series."

Trish had been telling us, in her usual headlong fashion, of how she had befriended, or been befriended by, an ailing guy named Thomas — since deceased — in Holyhead, of all places. "We first became friends," she said, "then lovers." She was well aware of the gradations, even though she was a stupid woman. And she was talking of an experience late in life, the hands crooked with arthritis and hardly all the better for feeling you with, the hair well into the later phases, no Rapunzel plaits there that he might climb without a stair. And the face? Well, OK; and as for the covered parts who'd know? This was no belated, rueful confession of a youthful indiscretion—this was what we have to call a relationship. There was no reason in the world why anybody but herself and Thomas would want to know anything about this Thomas, but that wouldn't keep her from telling, in elaborate detail, many of those things nobody wanted to know about him. And artfully slipping in that word to test further the reaction.

After all those years, one word and I suddenly realised how wrong I had been. The realisation gave me an empty and powerless feeling of adopted guilt, of knowing that a retrospective protestation of innocence was null and void and of no effect, as a lawyer might say. The guilt of having let myself be used, however unwittingly. And the guilt of not recognising that Danny, too, had been used. My studied neutrality had been manipulated into connivance; into acceptance of this serial adulteress as just another old pal, one of the gang. For if there was serial infidelity after that hasty marriage, what had she been up to before it? Had she ever had anything going for her but her bossy granting or withholding of sexual favours? And granting to how many?

There was nothing for it but to apologise to Danny for an offence of which he had been unaware, my offence in attributing to him an equal share of responsibility for the split and earlier, my acquiescence to the general acceptance of his paternity. Not easy stuff to phrase diplomatically and I pondered it in silence the next time we walked along the tow-path on our way to the village pub. The swans were still in residence and took off from the canal, their wing-tips whipping the water with powerful strokes until they were airborne, then filling the evening air with a strangely metallic beat.

It was an *Oíche shiamsa* in the pub, a music evening, and guitarists with parish-wide, if not county-wide, reputations were belting out Clancy Brothers' hits. 'Fine Girl You Are' was gleefully shouted and when the applause had died down the next per-

former, a slim young woman with dark hair and grey eyes, stilled
the resuming chatter with a sweet unwavering soprano as she
sang.

> *A story a story to you I'll relate*
> *Of a loving young damsel, oh sad was her fate.*
> *As she went a-Maying, a shower it had begun,*
> *She went under a bush, that shower for to shun.*
>
> *Jimmy went out fowling, with a gun in his hand,*
> *Fowling all day, as you may understand.*
> *His sweetheart being out walking, he took her for a swan,*
> *And he shot his Molly Bawn at the setting of the sun.*
>
> *Up spoke the great Councillor, his locks were grey,*
> *Saying 'Jimmy, my lad, do not think of going away;*
> *Stay in this country until your trial is on,*
> *And you never will be hanged for the shooting of a swan.'*
>
> *It was in three weeks after to her father she appeared,*
> *Saying 'Father, dearest father, don't let them hang my dear.*
> *He saw me through the bushes and me he took me for a swan,*
> *My white apron being around me, he shot his Molly Bawn.'*

"Follow that!" I said to myself, when her last note faded away.
Danny returned his lips to the rim of his glass, and sipped the
dark liquid as his eyes stayed studiously fixed on the middle of the
pint's froth crown. I knew full well that I could not now dredge
up with Danny those pallid jokes about *Swan Lake*, the midnight
skinny dipping, and the hiding of Trish's clothes, all that nonsense
at the old club's gala day; never mind the rushed marriage, the
rupture.

Next day, as I drove home, a dreadful stench assailed me, and
in a nearby field I saw a tractor, circling slowly. It was drawing a
tank sprouting long tubes with fine nozzles and through these
slurry was being sprayed and spread, a disgusting liquor of com-
minuted shit, including human waste.

Imagined monologues at a college function yield some explanation of the survival of the fittest

Director: *Fáilte romhaimh go léir go Gaillimh agus go dtí an cúrsa léinn seo. Tá mé cinte go bhfuil sibh go léir comh buíochden Uachtarán agus tá mé féin, as ucht a theacht anso chun fáiltiú romhaimh* ... the president ...

The president: ... I know a great deal has been done in the preparation of this course and I know from my recent happy visit to Boston College just how much your fellow-students there who attended previous courses in this series have valued the experience and I feel sure you will all benefit as much as did your predecessors. We are especially grateful to Prof. Weinberg for his continuing support of our joint ventures and perhaps it is not widely enough acknowledged that what he has done in bringing such groups as yourselves here is of great benefit to us. We are on the western fringe of Europe and three thousand miles from America and in a way proud of our insularity, but we realise that we need the stimulus and broadening of horizons which the presence of such a bright and forthcoming group as yourselves can bring ... *Guím rath ar bhur gcuid staidéir agus dar ndoigh ar bhúr gcuid caitheamh-aimsire freisin* ...

Prof. Weinberg, a little later, over drinks: ... I mean it's not in the same league. You take your faculty, your facilities, this beautiful riverside campus, it's got to have them beat. It's smaller, but that makes it that much more intimate, and so near the city, and there's that much going on; I mean in Cork last year all the kids could do was get a sixpack and a guitar and amuse themselves. Here you've two theatres, music venues where they can hear what you call *shanose* singing and people speaking Irish and they're so welcoming and I know these boys are going to find those Connemara colleens just knocking them out—and I'll be lucky if I can get all our girls to come home with me at the end of the course—those Connemara girls, all the Galway girls, are just so beautiful, I mean they talk about the trade with Spain and the Mediterranean look and I don't want to cast any slur on the morals of Spanish sailors or the girls in the Galway shawls, but there's got to be some explanation of the black hair, the grey eyes, the high cheek-bones, the perfect figures—jeez, the figures! ...

In another part of the room, an old Galway hand: But now listen to me, honey chile, as your coal-black mammy might have said if you'd come from a thousand miles farther south, you wouldn't want to put too much faith in what some of these academics tell you about Ireland, the terrible priest-ridden '30s and censorship and Puritanism, and how repressive and anti-intellectual it all was, and what a disgrace that Barnacle lassie from Bowling Green was that ran away with that Joyce that wrote the dirty books, and didn't even marry him, bould as you like. That's all for city folks, out in the townlands they had cocks and hens and bulls and cows and they knew all about the birds and the bees, and there was many a 'cousin,' if you hear the way I space it out with quotation marks, 'cousin' would you believe, was reared in a house out there in the Partry mountains with no uncle to account for them, all the result of a romp in the hay by the daughter of the house. The problem there wasn't that they were sheltered from sex; it was just that there weren't enough people to spread the burden around, the in-breeding was something fierce ... I remember driving a doctor to a patient up one of those narrow steep glens with a dead end, a box canyon I suppose you'd call it—I used to go fishing with him in one of the lakes up there—he warned me not to show surprise at anything I might see. Christ, if you saw the cut of a couple of the creatures up there, Othello's anthropophagi weren't in it with them, with their heads beneath their armpits or whatever it was ...

In yet another corner of the room, an assistant in the department of archaeology: You're steeped in luck this year, there's a rescue dig actually in progress quite near to town, usually the archaeology module of a summer course consists of loads of slides and a trip to a couple of sites in Aran ...

A student: Rescue dig?

Assistant: Yeah, that's what we call it, when a farmer or a quarryman or a developer or a road-gang or whatever comes across something they think we might be interested in, they're supposed to let us know and to hold off any further work that might damage the site, and most of them do, but we have to respond pretty sharpish because the delay costs them money, and if it looked as if it could cost them too much they might just bulldoze the whole bloody lot without saying a word to anybody. Anyway, this developer out in the suburbs had plenty of other areas to use his crew in, so we got a few weeks to dig what seems to be a cemetery, or maybe a *teampaillín*—

Student: A what?

Assistant: Sorry, I forgot you're only starting your Irish: it's the word for 'temple' with a diminutive added, like colleen and boreen, and 'little temple' is the euphemistic way of referring to a children's graveyard. Sometimes it's *raheen*, *rath* being the word for the old ring-fort, with the same 'een.' Probably unbaptized because they were furtively born, and furtively buried too, like the ones buried out on the mountainside where they caused the sods of the hungry grass to grow—God help the little mites, and the women that bore them, probably in an unfortunate situation. They came across masses of old bones, well you know what old means, could be any age longer ago than the people actually remember, like the famine, or some maybe medieval village that vanished or even genuine prehistoric. They're all infants' bones, fair enough, but the funny thing is their condition, all misshapen; I mean clavicles in a straight line that could never have let an arm swing, massive undershot jaws, feet with vestigial toes, twisted spines, legs without knees and femurs fused to tibia and fibula; you name it, it's there. I never saw such a collection, and apart altogether from the small corner that their bulldozer dug into before they noticed. And let me tell you one sweep of the shovels on those huge machines can do divil's own work altogether, there's a terrible lot of damage to the skeletons—and the doctor who was invited to see them before they decided it was a job for archaeology, he said he was pretty sure that most of the ones he could see anyway, if not all, had such signs of trauma, as he put it, that he was convinced they died by violence.

Topology and the hygienist

With a compendium of useless Victorian information

IT WAS A POSITION beyond the imaginings of the most acrobatic Brahmin in ancient India. She was behind me and told me to lie back. I did, and as I lay supine I found myself staring up at her, the back of my head cradled against her waist. In big close-up, I could see the swelling white of her bosom and on the left breast of her trim, starched overall an embroidered initial. Of course I was looking from below, so it could have been her right breast, and the initial could have been an M or a W. I couldn't see her face. There was nothing above or beyond that swelling bosom with its emblazoned M (or W) but a white cloth mask below dark eye-holes, they in their turn below a fringe of copper-tinted hair held by a thin white band.

Masque or Mask, I learn from the *National Encyclopaedia: a Dictionary of Universal Knowledge, by Writers of Eminence in Literature, Science, and Art* (London, Mackenzie, *n.d.,* [c. 1890]), was a species of drama which originated in the custom of enlivening processions and spectacles by the introduction of masked persons to represent imaginary characters.

I own a copy of vol. xi of this encyclopaedia, bringing me from the later stages of L—Lucifer, Luther and lycanthropy, for example (no offence meant)—to early Ns. These include Naturalism (in art and philosophy), Neo-Platonism, and an unfortunate essay *sub* Negro, wherein we learn that the cranial sutures close much earlier in the negro than in other races and many observers are disposed to find in this fact the reason for the marked mental inferiority of the race as compared with others. Which writer of eminence perpetrated this is not indicated, perhaps the same expert who told us that Malaria is a poison generated in soils the energies of which are not expended in the growth and sustenance of healthy vegetation. But Mind, Matter, Materialism, Memory, Muse, Manichaeism, Mirage, Mummers, Magic; are all there, treated with the same po-faced solemnity and condescension.

No imaginary character she, mask and all, M or W, no mummer, magician, nor mirage, but Material. Try mammary gland. Each orifice, would you believe, leads into a fine canal, which, however, soon dilates and ramifies with irregular and tortuous branches in the substance of the breast or udder. Hardly likely to whip up the old concupiscence, not to mention the unruly member. How different from the swelling bosom with its initial M or W.

W upside down is M and vice versa. Go further and the result of the following brief experiment may surprise you. The only equipment you need, apart from the book open before you as you read this, is a small hand-mirror such as comes as standard issue with ladies' handbags. Remain seated comfortably as you are and hold this mirror in your hand before you, at something less than arm's length, so that you may see your face in it. Now lower it so that its lower edge lands on this printed page just above and parallel to this line:

DICK HOCKED BIKE—CHIDED KID

You should be able to see that useless sentence reflected in your mirror and it will read there 'Dick hocked bike—chided kid.' No mirror image this, no reversal, no left for right, no top for bottom. Proof rather, if such were needed, of De Selby's cosmological *obiter dictum*, 'Everything is the same only upside down and backwards.'

The confusion of M and W, their interchangeability when viewed from above or below, was what originally exercised my mind as I lay there with my head against her soft waist and looked up at the M or W embroidered on the left (or right) breast of her virginal white smock. Write, for example, the word MOW and you will see WOM in your little mirror. For real confusion, try the other sort of mirror image. Write that silly sentence about dick and his bike on a piece of paper and hold it in front of you, facing your ordinary dressing-table mirror. What do you see in your mirror this time? Illegible, total garbage—but hold it facing the mirror *and upside down* and there is Dick, as clear and upright as ever, chiding that kid.

She was full of dire warnings about what would happen if I failed to follow her instructions. She even showed me, on a huge monitor screen, an image of the thin borderline between teeth and gums and yes, there it was; a yellow line of mould. Moulds, she explained, in terms reminiscent of the *National Encyclopaedia,* are constituted of fungi so small as to escape observation except when from their numbers they form microscopical forests, and then they clothe the surface of the body they attack with patches of yellow, blue, green ... Brushing of the teeth, she said, was an obsolete term. Massage the gums, she said, and the teeth will look after themselves.

She placed the end of a narrow tube in my open ("open big, please") mouth, so that its curled orifice hung in the dark valley between my lower gum and my cheek. It sucked the saliva and its accumulating alluvial deposits, and disposed of it, with some slobbering, through the sink-hole in the bottom of a cuspidor near my left elbow.

Her intellectual superiority over me was immediately manifest. As my imagination struggled to visualise Roman upper-case letters upside down and backwards, reversed, mirror-imaged, about-faced, she deftly inserted into my mouth a small mirror at the end of a short handle. Then, guided solely by images in that mirror of my teeth and of her probes, rasps, files and scrapers, she proceeded to probe, rasp, file and scrape my incisors, canines, molars, and premolars and the interstices between them. A builder's rubble, shards of calcified cement, clattered down to the valley between cheek and gum and was sucked thence through that gurgling hydraulic sump.

M or W was not wearing a mask or masque so that she could represent some imaginary character; nor was she wearing it to hide her identity, as might a terrorist or common stick-up artist. After all, she is prepared to flaunt a capital letter boldly on her left (or right) breast, presumably the initial of her forename. And the mask is not to protect me from her sweet and gentle exhalations. No, it is to protect herself against the breaths of patients which might be, betimes, anything but sweet and gentle. The spoil from her excavations of patients' teeth must on occasion be pretty offensive and I for one would never wish to commit such offence. I am only too happy, therefore, to go along with her suggestion of five brushings *per diem*: on rising, after breakfast, after lunch, after dinner, and on retiring.

The ancient Romans, by the way, ate Meals at quite different times, starting at five o'clock in the morning, or so I am informed by the *National Encyclopaedia.* It has, however, become necessary for a busy man to consider the amount of time that should be devoted to this mundane but obligatory task of tooth-brushing or gum-massaging. And to devise the most economical procedure.

For convenience let us agree that there are sixteen surfaces to be cleaned; the brush is to be moved across each surface many times (ten times is recommended) and then transferred to the next surface *with minimum travel.* The sixteen surfaces derive from human dentition, which has been elegantly described in a formula reading simply:

$$i \underline{2 - 2} \qquad c \underline{1 - 1} \qquad pm \underline{2-2} \qquad m \underline{3 - 3}$$

$$\underline{2 - 2} \qquad \underline{1 - 1} \qquad \underline{2-2} \qquad \underline{3 - 3}$$

The teeth are of equal length and approximating together, without intervals. The canines are short, so that there is no *diastema* or break in the teeth. (To what degree are many people unaware that this pattern of dentition is shared by Man with only one other species, the extinct artiodactyle ungulate Anoplotherium? Blissfully.)

OK. Front upper and lower teeth have sharp cutting edges and effectively only two sides, which we shall denominate outside (i.e. the lip side) and inside (i.e. the tongue side). Molars and premolars, the thicker lads at the back, above and below, left and right, have each three surfaces, outside (i.e. cheek side), inside (i.e.

tongue side), and top (i.e. grinding surface). Canines, pointy lads between cutters and grinders, will be deemed adequately brushed as neighbours front and rear are brushed.

OK so far?

Thus we have three surfaces, left and right, upper and lower, at the sides, total 2(3+3)=12; and two surfaces, upper and lower, at the front, total 2x2=4, overall total 16.

Brushing will be done horizontally, that is latterly, left-right-left-right. Some hygienists favour a vertical movement, as the more effectively removing food particles from the interstices between the teeth; radical ultras will insist on two full programmes, a vertical followed by a horizontal. The surfaces to be addressed and their logical order will be the same in both cases.

That order is as follows: front upper outside, left upper outside, left lower outside, front lower outside, right lower outside, right upper outside, right upper topside, right upper inside, front upper inside, left upper inside, left upper topside, left lower topside, left lower inside, front lower inside, right lower inside, right lower topside.

M or W recommends frequent replacement of the brush and at the end of each treatment gives the patient a present of a toothbrush hygienically wrapped in an unbroken plastic film. But perhaps I generalise and do myself less than justice; perhaps she doesn't give it to all patients. It could be a sign of some relationship between M or W and me which is becoming something a little more than merely professional.

M and W are used to distinguish between Men and Women, on spaces on architects' plans, for example, which indicate where toilets for Men and Women are to be installed. She is as clearly a W as I am an M. That bosom, this member. But Madonna or Whore, Wendy or Mandy, Maurice or Michael, Winnie or Minnie or Mavis or Molly or Mona or Wilfred or Mildred or Wally or Warren or William … The article on Matrimony is a dull recitation of legalisms from classical and modern sources, with little regard for love or even sex.

There is no entry for Mating.

Here's their memory

IF WE HAD EVER heard the word, we would have had to agree that our family was among the *literati* of Rathbeggan. My father was a solicitor's clerk, his mother was — had been — a teacher for a length of time 'out of the mind of man,' as the saying goes. I first knew her as an elderly lady, slightly stooped, who walked with the assistance of a cane. When finally seated, she would charm a grandson with droll accounts of times past — a death or a wedding in the neighbourhood, a local report of some distant achievement by one of our many local exiles — these were enough to prompt her flow of kindly anecdotes; always linked, in good teacherly fashion, to the shop or the house or the person that she knew was familiar to me, her young audience. The teacherly manner, alas, was not to last. With advancing age, though her memory of incidents survived, her recall of details faltered, and eventually she was telling me of "the one across the road there, you know the woman that had the shop, well, she was the one, before she married that other chap, the fellow whose brother was the doctor in Dublin, he used always come here on holidays ..." By this stage I was wishing that I had taken notes of her earlier lucid narratives. But what's missed stays missed.

Between us, she and I spanned more than a century, the miserable twentieth. She was born in the closing decade of the nineteenth, and here was I, editor of the town's only newspaper, wondering how to join in marking 2006 as the ninetieth anniversary of 1916.

My father was a solicitor's clerk, owing a brief exposure to classical learning, which gained him his post, to an equally brief notion that his future lay in holy orders. The solicitor for whom he clerked was not a resident, and visited Rathbeggan only on a certain day each week and to attend at court when held here. So my father ran the office day to day and was eventually, for convenience in preparing proceedings, admitted one of those commissioned for the taking of oaths in the court of this, that or the other. He was a person, that is to say, before whom affidavits might be sworn. (It was no great distinction; there were a couple of thousand of them throughout the country.) Like his mother, he was a repository of facts about many of the neighbours whom we greeted in the street every day, but, unlike his mother, he was precluded by the ethics of his business from revealing any part of this private knowledge. He had merely been heard to remark once that "You'd be very surprised the things people hereabouts have had to swear oaths about." Needless to say, there were few openings for a lad with a bookish background in our sleepy little town in the sleepy decades after World War Two and I have to admit that there was a 'word in your ear' to the editor-proprietor of our weekly paper, who happened to be a friend of the clerk running the local solicitor's office. As a result of this collusion among the *literati* of Rathbeggan I was recruited to the staff of the *Midlands Topic*, as chief (and only) sub-editor, chief (and only) reporter, tea-maker, advertising canvasser, and (when I cycled to the neighbouring town where there was a jobbing house) printer's devil.

The muted observances proposed for this year, 2006, marking that anniversary of Easter Week, 1916, forced me to recall the more flamboyant celebrations of what might well be called the golden jubilee of the rising, in 1966. I had just started work here as a cub reporter—deaths of local worthies and their funerals, congratulations to officials about to retire, successes of persons of local origin in the distant business or entertainment worlds of Dublin—these were the things a cub reporter was expected, and paid, to write about. The editor himself, on whose chair I now sit, that very chair with the bare spot on the left arm-rest's upholstery where his Parkinsonian tremor constantly rubbed, he himself continued to write reports on the UDC, on planning issues which were just beginning to heat up, on splits and coalitions between and within local branches of the main national political parties. But mad anxious to prove and improve myself, I marched in to the editor and said:

"Can I suggest something for this 1916 commemoration that's going on everywhere?"

"Like what?" he asked.

"Well," I explained, "wouldn't it be an idea to get all the kids in the local schools to talk to their gran'mas and gran'das and so on to ask them what they remember about 1916 and the War of Independence and we could offer a prize—?"

He held up his hand and when I paused, replied soothingly:

"Now lookit, son, there's to be army parades and pageants to beat the band above in Dublin, and down here the UDC is going, to my certain knowledge, all parties agreeing for a change, to erect a memorial which I think will be a plaque on the bridge below there, in memory of all who died or maybe even just fought for Ireland and we'll cover all that with photographs and all and that'll do us to be going on with. I know you meant well but there's some of the older folk around here wouldn't want anyone writing down whatever it is they remember of those troubled times." "But," I persisted with the pig-headed persistence of youth, "wouldn't it be a good idea, before these ... "

"Well, now, lad, I'll tell you something. I've a brother who was a Guard, he's retired now, and he was stationed off out there in the west end of Connemara, a place where all the men were rotten with poteen from one year's end to the other, and there was a priest came to give the Mission and he knew about the scandalous amount of deadly illicit drink that was getting made and drunk and he preached against it, asking for a bonfire of vanities, he called it; the men were to bring in all the distilling equipment and they'd make a huge bonfire of it inside the church gate. And indeed they did, exceptin' that my brother knew something that that poor innocent Redemptorist didn't—who wouldn't have known the difference between the worm of a still and a broken piece of any banjaxed old bicycle and who had no idea that there was changes in the distilling business, it was just after the war and bottled gas was coming in and metal barrels—so the poor missioner put a match to the pile of barrel-staves and twisted bits of obsolete farm machinery, and he was delighted with himself, and they were as mad drunk as ever the next week-end after he left, and I don't know why that episode came into my head, but it shows that things are often not what they seem to be, 'specially when a crowd of people close ranks. And there's all sorts of reasons why people should close ranks, and there's still very hard feelin's around—on all sides. I suppose you've come across John Kells Ingram?" he concluded, with seeming irrelevance.

"Of course," I replied, "'Who fears to speak of ninety-eight?'; Trinity and all that."

"Yes, well," the editor resumed, "that's what people mostly call it but it's not the proper title, it's just the first line—do you know the verse beginning 'Here's their memory?'"

I shook my head.

"It was 1848 and he was commemorating the fiftieth anniversary of the rising of 1798, just like your men above in Dublin are celebrating the fiftieth anniversary of 1916, and he was proposing a toast to the memory of the dead, and that's the title of the song, but let me tell you there's memories and memories in it and there's people around here wouldn't thank you for searching them out."

The great oral history idea I had put before my editor that spring, 1966, was not really as original as I made out. My grandmother had been one of the generation of school-teachers who had been invited by the Folklore Commission to organise the collection by the schoolchildren of all sorts of local lore from their elders—crafts, curses and cures, seasonal observations and saints' days, holidays and holy days, patterns, processions, popular prayers, fairy forts and faction fights, factual or fictional local heroes, traditional songs and tales, practices and beliefs about birth, marriage and death—all the invisible conventions which bind the community together and which nobody bothers to write down because everybody knows them. She treasured a letter in Irish which she had received from Prof. Delargy, head of the Folklore Commission, complimenting her on the excellence of the collections made by the children in her school.

From the summit of the small eminence, which is the highest point in the county, one could see, it was said, more counties than from any other viewpoint in Ireland. Certainly, on a clear day, there was visible to the west, across a vast acreage of bog, the sheen of the Shannon on the far horizon; and to the east, the humps of hills in Wicklow and Dublin. The village of Togher, a huddle of about twenty small houses, mostly thatched, slumbered on in its dark street between that hill and the long summit level of a canal—a canal surveyed, dug, puddled, embanked and watered just ahead of the expanding railways which made it obsolete almost before it opened to traffic.

Thus the opening of the covering description my mother wrote for Prof. Delargy to accompany the children's collections. A little flowery, perhaps, but elegant enough, and depicting clearly one of the more remote villages in her school's catchment. (She told me that she had continued the writing of her locality's history in the form of a personal memoir, but had never completed it and I never found it among her papers.)

Facts that remain unspoken still manage to be propagated round a country town and so I was not really surprised when I was accosted a few days after my chat with the editor by an acquaintance—no more—an elderly guy with a shock of white hair, as I sat minding my own business in a local pub.

"So you're collecting the history of the old IRA?" he asked.

"Not exactly," I replied, "but that'll do to be going on with. How did you know?"

"'Never mind that now, I have something to tell you that you won't find in any history book, and it's a true bill."

"Good man," I said, "tell us all."

"My uncle Dermot," he began, "was out in the Troubles, and one day—he told me this his own self and swore me to secrecy and I never told a soul as long as he was alive, but they're all dead now, Tans and IRA men and all, so I can tell it now after all this time—he was out anyway and one day the Black and Tans came to Rathbeggan in a couple of lorries and did the usual thing; burnt down a few shops, fired their guns through a few windows. It must have been after the sergeant was shot in the barracks when the other RIC men were at Mass, anyway the Tans came as I was saying, and most of the young lads had legged it out of the place

that might have been liable to be taken by the Tans for being sus-
pected of being in the IRA, my uncle last of all to leave, he was a
bit younger than the others, he was only just out of the Fianna
Éireann, that was the kind of boy scouts they had, for preparing
lads, like, for the real business of being in the IRA proper; anyway,
he was behind the lot of them and he saw all that happened after.
So the Tans apparently thought they were owed a few drinks and
they occupied this very pub we're sitting in now — it was Larkin's
then, but it was a young Larkin girl that married one of the
O'Briens that was the daddy of young Tom O'Brien that's here
now, but never mind all that, they occupied it anyway, except two
officers who wandered off, I suppose they didn't want to know
what their lads might get up to, anyway they came the same direction my uncle Dermot was going off in, and they got so close
he had to hide himself by climbing up a tree because there was
only open ground beyond where he'd be seen, and bedamn but
didn't me two Tan officers sit down under the same tree, smoking
and chatting about the war and all, and how they'd been in
trenches near one another in the war, and patrols in No Man's
Land, and over the top and the Somme, and what should have
been done and wasn't, and what the Hun did next and one of
them says 'And the next move should have been . . .' when the other guy interrupts and says, 'You've just reminded me, wasn't it
your move?' and bedamn doesn't he take out of his haversack a
portable draughtsboard with little holes bored in it in the middle
of each square and a chess set with pieces that had little pegs in
the bottom so they'd fit steady in the little holes in the board, do
you understand me?, and sets up the chessmen like it was the
middle of a game! Now uncle Dermot sees and remembers all this
because isn't he the schoolboys champion of chess in the whole
province of Leinster? And one of your men below is in a very tight
spot, with his queen *en prise*, as they say, and if he moves her
doesn't he give the other man a move in hand, but begod there's
one clever little move on the other side of the board that'll give
him a counter-threat but it looks as if he's not going to see it and
my uncle Dermot is mad anxious to show off that he's seen it, but

of course he daren't move or speak, so what does he do but take a nut or a berry or whatever it was off his tree and drop it down smack on the square that your man below should move his pawn to and he looks at the square and then looks up at his opponent and says, 'B'God, man, I nearly missed that,' and he makes the move and goes on to win—checkmates him! And they pack up their board and go back down to the town and my uncle Dermot claims that that move got known as the Tan's king's knight's pawn gambit, but I'm not sure about that last bit, I think he was boasting; now isn't that a queer one for your collection? And he swore me to secrecy because he was afraid people would think the less of him for giving aid and comfort to the enemy, even if they were only playing chess." Like that man's chess-playing uncle Dermot, all the first-hand informants who had survived to 1966 had passed away by 2006 and we're left with *dúirt-bean-liom-go-ndúirt-bean-léi* and what became in the telling three black crows turns out to have been just something as black as a crow. I can still feel the pang of disappointment at the failure of my great idea all those years ago, especially when our columns dutifully recite the national record, as it's called, of some local politician when he passes away. The son of one such white-haired veteran, drinking with me after his father's funeral, told me in strictest confidence a story his father had told, when he too was in his cups. Following some Black-and-Tan outrage, word came from Collins that there was to be an action against enemy forces in every brigade area the next weekend. The boys in Rathbeggan had so far contented themselves with chopping down a few trees to disrupt His Majesty's Mails and had to think of something more militant. They fixed on the RIC barracks, one of the few still open around the country, with a small complement of constables, a couple of them married locally, and a sergeant in charge. A small boy—I suspect it was the deceased white-haired patriot, but we'll never know—gave the signal to the IRA when all the constables had gone to Mass on the Sunday morning, and the IRA's active service unit, the ASU as it was called, the flying column, went in and shot the sergeant dead.

If all those white-haired patriots are now dead, there is still a
resource which will make good the loss their passing may represent. As the last of them die off, the government can now release
the statements which a national specialised body collected, to
cover military aspects of the modern fight for Irish freedom. The
bibulous gossip of my friend's late white-haired parent may be
stilled but as one of the more pompous of my English teachers
pointed out, *Litera scripta manet, verbum imbelle perit*; which I
make so bold as to translate: *The spoken word is weak and dies,
what's written down is what survives.* (Even if it's bloody lies.)

```
STATEMENT
Office use only
Gnó oifige amháin
Uimh. BSM
Capt. Victor SPILLANE, 'A' coy.,
Rathbeggan battalion, Midland brigade, IRA,
Aug. 1919-1924.
```

My family home was in the village of Togher but I
spent most of my adult life in the town of Rathbeggan.

I was officer commanding an ASU [Active Service
Unit] with members selected from the local companies
of the [Rathbeggan battalion of the] Republican Army.
We were actively engaged in attacks on communications during late 1919 and 1920, in particular attacks on transport facilities in regular use by the
enemy or Crown forces, which had committed several
outrages in the locality. Our IO [Intelligence Offi-
cer] identified the Rathbeggan RIC barracks, one of
the few remaining open and manned, as the centre for
the distribution of the enemy's counter-intelli-
gence. An encirclement of the barracks was effected
in company strength on Sunday 21 Jan. 1921 and sus-
tained fire was opened on this enemy strongpoint at
1105 hours, and heavy casualties inflicted on the

British occupying force.

Following the acceptance of the Treaty by Dáil Éireann I joined the national army and was commissioned and served several years, as the official record will show.

AFFIDAVIT
Office use only
Gnó oifige amháin
Uimh. BSM
Vol. Dermot LARKIN, 'C' coy.,
Rathbeggan Battalion, 1920-21

I was a member of the ASU selected from the companies of the Rathbeggan battalion. We were actively engaged in attacks on communications during late 1919 and 1920, including attacks on transport facilities in regular use by the enemy forces which had committed several outrages in the locality. Our spies identified the local RIC barracks as a centre for the enemy's information system. It was surrounded and fired upon on Sunday 2 Jan. 1921 and heavy casualties inflicted.

Office use only
Gnó oifige amháin
Uimh. BSM
AFFIDAVIT
of Daniel O'Brien of 29 Mill Street,
Newton, Mass., made before me Robert O'Neill,
Attorney-at-law, Licensed by
the Supreme Court of the Commonwealth of Massachusetts for the taking of oaths.

I Robert O'Neill, attorney-at-law, hereby certify and declare that the following deposition was made

before me on the eighth day of August 1942 by Daniel
O'Brien of 29 Mill Street, Newton, in the state of
Massachusetts and duly signed and attested by him in
the presence of Matilda Hodgson, clerk, and that I
know the deponent.

My name is Daniel O'Brien, I was born and reared in
the town of Rathbeggan in Ireland where I was known
as Domhnall. I learn from a report in the Irish Sham-
rock that the government in Ireland has set up a Bu-
reau to gather statements from people who were out
in the Troubles, as we used to say. I came to this
country because if I stayed at home I would have been
faced with imprisonment or worse. After four years
of war, the Irish Republican Army, with shotguns for
shooting crows, sporting miniature rifles for hunting
rabbits, aye that and rosary beads in their hands,
had brought to its knees a force of thousands of
blood-thirsty ex-officers of the British army, brought
to Ireland as Auxiliary police or as a military force
with such an assortment of uniforms that we called
them the Black and Tans, after a famous pack of
hounds. And after that they offered us a treaty which
cut the country in two and left us all still in the
British Empire and taking oaths of loyalty to the
British crown. Some of us weren't having any of this
and when the so-called Free State government began
putting true republicans in jail, those of us who had
the chance took it and came on the first available
boat to this great country. This country knows what
it is to fight against the tyranny of a foreign king,
knows what it is to fight for freedom, just as my two
sons are fighting for freedom in the Pacific at this
very moment. I'm sorry Mr. O'Neill, should I leave
all that in? Maybe I've been a bit over the top? Yes,
I think so, we can look at it again later. [Miss

Hodgson's shorthand notes and transcript] Before
that miserable civil war we had been quite a useful
squad, they called us an ASU or Active Service Unit
and, jokingly, a flying column. We chopped down trees
to block the railway line one time, to stop the de-
livery of all those pensions to retired British army
types. And that reminds me, there were active re-
cruiters for the British all through that time, well
up to the end of 1918 anyway. We were putting a scare
into one of them, the local doctor—a real Irish Par-
liamentary Party type, would have followed Redmond
into hell—when things went badly wrong. Vincent
Spillane was the OC [Officer Commanding] of the ASU
and he told us the brigade IO [Intelligence Officer]
had checked right back along and found that it was
this doctor that was behind the education in Dublin
of a young chap from the town, Tom Holt, and his
joining the British army there. He got some decora-
tion for his efforts and stayed in England after being demobbed, and we never saw him again. But there
was no doubt about the doctor's sympathy for the
British up to and after 1918. We were all wearing
masks during his interrogation, 'cause he'd readily
recognise us all, and at one stage he suddenly shouted, "I know all your voices, you can take your silly
masks off!" He stood up and made a swipe as if to
pull the mask off Vic—no, his name wasn't Vincent—
anyway the doctor made this swipe and Vincent—no,
Victor—lashed at him with his pistol and the doctor
fell down. Dead. He must have had a heart attack or
something. We'd a quick conference and decided there
was nothing we could do about it so Vic fired a bul-
let into him and we left his body with the usual
warning pinned to his chest: 'spies and informers
beware.' I know he wasn't a spy or informer, just a
recruiter, but we used him to make an example any-

way. Another day we eliminated the RIC barracks, which was a nest of spies. Somebody sent me a cutting about this from a local paper and I'm adding a copy of it.

DR. CORCORAN FOUND SHOT
MURDER OF POPULAR LOCAL FIGURE

Outrage was expressed in Rathbeggan last Tuesday when the public learned that the body of a man, shot dead, and furnished with a note in a manner becoming all too familiar had been identified as that of Dr. Conor Corcoran, medical officer, who had an extensive practice in Rathbeggan and surrounding areas. The note pinned to his clothing repeated a warning to 'spies and informers,' implying that the unfortunate victim had been guilty of some action which had raised the ire of those who are at present wandering throughout the county armed to the teeth with deadly weapons and no apparent purpose other than the murder and intimidation of innocent citizens. The deceased was a moderate nationalist who took no active part in the politics of party wrangling but nevertheless gave a lead in true democracy by selfless public service to the community irrespective of class and creed.

He is survived by his wife Joan and his daughter Monica.

MIDLANDS TOPIC 31.08.1920

It was the hand of that kindly old editor, and not mine, which wrote the obituary on Councillor Spillane, chairman of the Urban District Council and local representative of a major Dublin insurance company.

Councillor Victor Spillane, who died last week, 27th ult., at an advanced age and after a prolonged and worthy battle with the grim reaper armed with the dread disease cancer, which the medical fraternity have come to regard as one of the worst killers known, was no stranger to the risk of Death. Born in the village of Togher, he spent much of his early life there,

*travelling ten miles every day on his bicycle to pursue his edu-
cation at St. Agatha's in the town of Rathbeggan, where he
was to spend most of his adult life. He early enrolled there in
Óglaigh na hÉireann and had often in his youth returned the
basilisk stare of the skeleton which hovered beside them, as
Captain Spillane and his comrades in the local Active Service
Unit lay silent and cold on the roadside preparing to ambush
the trucks of drunken Black and Tans, the dregs of Britain's
military prisons, as they rampaged around the country on
their dread missions, looting shops, burning down co-ops, fir-
ing their weapons indiscriminately, causing injury and even
death to innocent civilians, including women and children
and otherwise attempting to stifle the emerging national identity of a free Ireland. When a treaty brought an end to these
international military manoeuvres, the terms of the settlement
were disputed and led to a brief civil war. Young Victor Spillane quickly left the military scene and set about building a ca-
reer for himself in the new nation. Long prominent in the insurance business, he had interests in other industries as well
and served on several government-appointed commissions and
represented the insurance industry at several international
conferences. He first stood for election to the local authority as
the nominee of the short-lived United Ireland party, and after
that party's amalgamation with the present major opposition
party, Victor Spillane was elected first to the UDC, then to the
county council, and finally to Dáil Éireann. There he served
only one term and spent the rest of his life looking after local
interests throughout this county on his own behalf and on behalf of numerous applicants for his advice and assistance, of
which he always gave generously. He was chairman of the
committee of the local GAA club and gave equally generously
of his time to other public undertakings. As we reported in our
last issue, an overflow crowd attended his obsequies, and at the
solemn funeral Mass in St. Agatha's, Mons. Diarmuid El-
wood, P.P., V.F., in a moving allocution on the inevitability
of death and hope in the hereafter, paid tribute to the steadfast*

faith of Victor Spillane, a pillar of the community and a stal-
wart supporter of the church. Votes of sympathy on his death
have been passed at meetings of a number of public bodies
since news of his passing spread.

"They tell me," my grandmother said, "that that man died, that
had that little insurance office on the Tullamore Road. Somebody
told me what it said in the paper about him and it wasn't a bit like
that at all; I knew the girl well she was a bit younger than me but
we were pals and she told me all about it, she had a bicycle that
was very advanced for those days, I never had one until I got the
job teaching there, but she had a bike because her daddy was so
very advanced, he had a motor car and of course he was pretty
wealthy compared to the rest of us, and of course Victor had a bicycle too, because he had to come all the way to school from that
horrible little village out there in the bog, it must have been all of
five miles, and anyway to avoid passing the doctor's house, which
was one of those stone houses with steps up up there at the top of
the town, they'd take the old line road after school on their bikes
and it was all perfectly innocent, I don't think it went as far as a
kiss or even holding hands, but one day and she never forgot it,
they were out at the Togher end of the old line and she was so em-
barrassed she had to excuse herself and left him holding the two
bikes when she went into the bushes, and just as she was coming
back through the gap to the road the doctor comes by in his mo-
tor-car in a cloud of dust and sees her and stops and gets out
shouting at her, calling her a brazen hussy and telling her to get
into the motor and never mind her 'bloody' bike, and to Spillane
he says, 'I'll have something to say to your parents and don't you
dare ever to speak to my daughter again.' But of course all he got
out of Victor's parents was a bit of a laugh so he spoke to the cler-
gy and they were read out at Mass, well not exactly, but the priest
condemned young fellows from other places coming into the
town and corrupting young women of gentler rearing, and everybody knew who he meant, and the young curate who was chap-
lain to the school Father—you know the man I mean, he was

over in that other place later on — told them about the dangers of
company-keeping and young men's passions being so easily
aroused and young women being exposed to the dangers of modern life like bicycling, would you believe it, and Victor who hated
the village of Togher already, with its damp smoky cottages, now
hated the school and the church as well and the town and the
doctor ..."

Squitlings of memory or imagination on the Upper Shannon

eath

scrib

"IT'S A LONG TIME NOW," the sergeant was saying, "since they made jokes about us having little notebooks and little stubs of pencils; 'do you mind if we haul this body you found in Exchequer Street round the corner into Dame Street?'—that kind of thing. Now it's all computers. And this yoke," he concluded, with a heavy slap on the side of the cardboard crate as he unpacked the shredder and placed it squarely on its papercatcher basket.

He picked up a few sheets of A4, riffled them and tapped them edge downwards on the table until edges and ends were even, plugged the lead from the shredder into a wall-socket, pressed two switches on the machine and presented the gathering of leaves to a slot on the top. Obligingly, the shredder coughed into life, swallowed the sheets gradually into its maw, and stopped as suddenly. The sergeant lifted the heavy shredding unit off its basket and took from the plastic bag in its interior a fistful of the tiny fragments it had produced.

"There's a cheaper job," he explained, "that only cuts your stuff into long strips like streamers, there's a second blade in this one that chops crossways and makes this stuff like confetti. Hardly a word to be read." The other Guards crowded round the machine, picking up odd sheaves of paper to try it.

"Now for Chrissake," the sergeant continued, "be careful of this yoke and how you use it, it's for disposal of unwanted paper—we've got to be absolutely bloody certain sure we're never,

ever, ever going to need a piece of paper again before we shred it, and make sure the copy you're shredding is a copy and not the original. If the bloody wigs ever get to hear that one single wrong shredding has been done we'll never hear the end of it."

"'Is it not a fact then, Guard,'" he mimicked, "'that certain documents in your station were shredded? And would you not agree, Guard, that destruction of documents puts an unnecessary strain on ordinary human memory? We cannot be sure, can we, Guard, that in relying on memory alone we are claiming to recall certain facts accurately when we do not have in confirmation the support of contemporary documents now reduced to useless little squitlings of waste paper? And without that evidential support, Guard, are we not entirely dependent on memory? And memory can be so fallible, can it not? — Or perhaps in some cases I should call it imagination …'"

To his surprise, he saw the odd word or near-word here and there. Picking up a few of the short fragments and peering at them, he read aloud: "stat, epor, t space ex, ith — see what I mean?"

When the others had left the day-room, he started taking old papers out of his desk. Many of them were multiple 'Photostat' copies, smudgy black and white, of documents circulated in the course of investigations long finished — or abandoned. He paused over one, a grisly portrait of a corpse. He remembered the case, though it was thirty years since he had been sent, as a young Guard, to supervise the recovery of that young man's body from reed beds below Knockvicar. There it had been discovered by a horrified angler whose cast had foul-hooked the tattered remains of something like battle-dress.

The soot-and-chalk 'Photostat' image failed utterly to convey the sickening ugliness of a bloated white, dead white, face, nibbled by rats or fish.

And the maggots, he recalled with a shudder, had been removed before the photograph was taken, so as not to interfere with possible recognition. Must have been floating with the face above water for a while, or do some flies lay their eggs and have them hatch out all under water? Should have asked about that. Battle-dress? "Don't rush to conclusions," his sergeant had advised, "there's lots of young fellows like to wear army surplus these days."

Never identified, nobody reported missing, no record of man overboard in the dozens of hired cruisers and privately-owned craft which had motored through this reach over two or three weeks, nobody had witnessed a suicide or drowning.

He couldn't remember where or when he had picked up the U.S. War Department field manual of criminal investigation, its pages now browning round the edges. Printed 1945, war-time paper. Shred? The rawest counsel could make any witness quoting it look foolish. "Are you aware, Guard, of how many editions of this manual, subsequent to that of 1945, have been issued by the U.S. War Department—let me tell you, then, Guard, seven, all of seven newer editions ..."

A page caught his eye as he tore the book apart for feeding into the shredder.

'*EXAMINATION OF BODIES* It is suggested that the examination of the body begin at the head, observing the head covering, if any, and the colour, length, arrangement and contents of the hair. Observe the face for injuries, blood, dirt, extraneous matter, distinctive marks, the position of the eyes and mouth, and the expression. ... Matter under the fingernails may be removed for analysis. The clothing of the body should be noted for its arrangement or disarrangement, degree of cleanliness ... its material, quality, color, pattern, and name of maker ...'

All too easy—eyes and mouth in the normal position, more or less. A few longwinding wisps of dark hair, a few tattered rags of underwear, about the shoulders the remains of a camouflage jacket, in green with patches of orange and brown, the label, happily surviving, and recording that the maker or supplier was Millets, the well-known outdoor gear shop.

'When handling cadavers the investigator should use rubber gloves to prevent septic poisoning. (a) Deceased persons may be fingerprinted as follows: ... (c) When the body has been in water for a considerable period of time, the fingers are invariably in such a wrinkled condition that fingerprinting is impossible without first preparing the fingers by removing the wrinkles. An injection of tissue builder ... the skin may be removed with a scalpel. It should then be immersed in alcohol ... for drying and hardening. Using rubber gloves, place the hardened skin around the investigator's own finger and make a regular rolled fingerprint impression. (d) If the deceased's fingers are in an advanced state of decomposition, they may be amputated, dried and photographed ...'

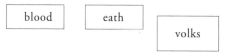

The plastic bag for cut paper was now nearly full and he removed the heavy head of the shredder. He ran his fingers through the soft pile of scraps and to his surprise saw the odd word or near-word here and there:

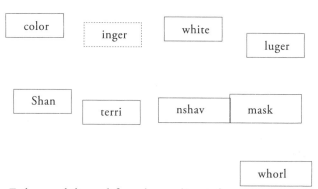

Erika was bilingual from her earliest infancy, her mother always spoke Polish to her, her father German. Her parents had married a few years after the war and as a teenager she had witnessed the hard work in cold and hunger which had created the *Wirtschaftwonderland*. She left the *Gymnasium* with many credits, especially for languages, and after studies in Germany became a postgraduate scholar at the Dublin Institute for Advanced Stud-

ies and spent some time in Irish-speaking areas and in the Gàid-
healtachd of Scotland. But life was not all comparative linguistics

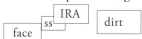

and she came to enjoy what her Irish fellow-scholars called the
'craic.' And thus it was that she persuaded her father and mother
to join her on a hired cruiser, for a week on the Shannon.

They met by arrangement at Carrick, where they were to take
command of their boat, and as they approached the jetty clamor-
ous small boys selling bait were finally silenced only when Ulrich
parted with unfamiliar Irish coins for a jam-jar full of squirming
yellow maggots.

"There's a rod all ready on board," the boat-hire company's
agent remarked, as he began a few minutes instruction on boat
handling, enough to send them on their way. Erika's father, Ulrich, at the wheel, with his hand on the throttle, exclaimed that it
was just like driving a tank.

cloth

"Forward, reverse, faster, slower, turn left, turn right. It's the
same smell, too," he said, "and that blue smoke puffing from the
exhaust is just the same." But this was peaceful riding, as, trailing
a small dinghy astern, *Medusa* chugged steadily forward, head of
an arrow of wavelets spreading from the prow, breaking into the
restless water of the small lakes they crossed; mere widenings of
the Shannon's course. Little gasping splash-points here and there

aclava

created bubbles which died on the instant, leaving glistening
white streaks on the dark slopes of ripples, reticulated scuds
brushing the water and vanishing.

Ulrich was tall, blond and handsome, though for some years
the term "blond" had been a charitable one to apply to a greying
and thinning frizzle. He spoke English well; as a tall blond smiling schoolboy he had been sent on a goodwill exchange mission
to the United States in the mid-30s, but only because his appearance satisfied the racist preoccupation of the authorities. At short
notice, they had had to find a replacement for a local *alte Kämp-*

fer's son, who had been first choice for the mission but had been taken ill as his departure date approached.

The long day's objective was Lough Key—Ulrich laughed to himself, secretly proud of his grasp of English and of the unconscious pun in the name. But before that they had to familiarise themselves with the buoys and perches marking the safe channel—upstream, red markers to left—and to negotiate their first lock; its weir, chamber and gates taming a shoaled drop in the natural course of the river.

The tail-gate was closed as they approached and they stopped well clear of the massive entrance, and threw a loop of line to an obliging bystander, who dropped it over a bollard. The boat was held safe as racks were opened and water rushed from the emptying lock-chamber. The rush eased and stopped, the tail-gate swung slowly open and a small flotilla of downstream boats emerged. Ulrich, commanding *Medusa* and feeling like a genuine *Kapitän zur see,* led four upstream crafts into the chamber, the tailgate closed behind them, and, safety warps again looped around bollards, the boats rose as upstream racks were opened to fill the chamber. The flow eased, the headgate swung slowly wide and the upstream craft motored safely towards the lake.

Medusa's crew of three agreed that there was enough daylight time left to allow them to take a brief respite from the unfamiliar tasks involved in working the boat, and they tied up to the bank in the quiet wide stretch between the lock and the lake. Hania, always the *gute Hausfrau,* set about making coffee in a constricted galley space; and Ulrich took the ready-mounted fishing rod from its clips on the canopy, baiting the hook with a maggot. In gingerly fashion he swung the rod and released the line so that the baited hook, a small weight and a quill float drew monofilament off the reel, ran out and dropped the lure in deep water. He watched his float drift slowly downstream with the current and left the rod propped firmly against the bow-rail when his wife called "*fertig!*" When he returned a few minutes later, coffee cup in hand, the tip of the rod was curved towards the water and the line was taut and slanting steeply, the float well sunk. Excited at his success, he reeled in carefully and felt the sudden flurry of strong life at the end of the line. His unexpected prize was a golden panting jack pike, bending and twisting on the narrow deck. Unfamiliar with the ways of anglers, he was unable to release the hook from his catch's vicious mouth or throat, and after a few bloody attempts, decided that the merciful thing to do was to dispatch it as quickly as possible. As it lay on the hard deck, a sudden blow of the edge of his hand held rigid, striking between head and body, caused one weak flap of the tail fins, and the fish died. With some distaste and regret, he dumped the dead thing in the river as they untied from the bank and motored on into Lough Key.

They found a mooring at a small jetty, little frequented but convenient for the brisk walk, with steadier legs, to the town of Boyle. There a pub-grub evening meal was followed by what Erika explained to her parents was 'the craic.' A local enthusiast interspersed good-natured banter at the expense of visitors and natives alike with raucous balladry to the accompaniment of a severely limited number of chords strummed on guitar. In high good humour, 'Fine girl you are' still ringing in their ears, they stepped out towards their jetty along roads dark as only country roads can be, overshadowed by trees on a moonless night. Carrying a torch against such an eventuality, Erika flashed her beam on the narrow walkway of the jetty, then on the wheelhouse of *Medusa*.

As she stepped aboard, a voice grated from the short companionway: "Put out that light and keep coming, or I'll shoot." She stopped suddenly, immobilised by shock at what she had heard. Ulrich and Hania, aware that something had been said, but failing to follow what was unexpected and unfamiliar, crowded behind the frozen figure of their daughter.

Now a hoarse shout: "Come on, COME ON! Put out that light and stay quiet, I have a gun." A final swing of her torch showed Erika that the dark figure below seemed indeed to have a pistol in his hand; she switched off the torch and the three of them stepped timorously into the wheel-house.

"Please don't shoot," she urged, "they don't understand English."

An inspired lie, uttered in the hope of maintaining a means of communication secret from their menacing super-cargo.

"Tie down those canopy things, awnings," the gunman ordered.

She spoke briefly in German and her father replied gruffly, the voice from the companionway retorting: "I don't speak German, but I recognise it when I hear it, and I heard that man say 'terrorist.' I'm no terrorist, I'm a soldier of the Irish Republic."

"What do you want then?" Erika asked.

"I want to free my country from foreign government and foreign armed forces and get back the land that was stolen from us by Orange bastards three hundred years ago."

"I mean what do you want from us here? We've very little money, only travellers cheques."

"I'm not a robber, if that's what you mean, I came on to your boat looking for food; I've been walking the hills for two nights without any. I can see you against the sky clear enough to shoot: one of you pull up that hood behind you and switch on some light, there's got to be a light from a battery or something in a boat like this." Erika undid the ties holding the wheelhouse hood, and turned a light switch on the dash in front of the wheel. Now they could see the figure crouched on the companionway, the dark-blue steel of the flat automatic in his hand — a Luger, Ulrich thought — the blotched camouflage jacket and, most frightening, the woollen sock pulled over his head like a balaclava, with roughly torn holes for his eyes.

She had heard of an engagement at Florencecourt, just over the border in Co. Tyrone, where a party of armed republicans had attacked a fortified police station. Their fire had been returned and they were reported to have withdrawn and been pursued as far as the Border by a British army unit. Their stowaway, she guessed, was one of those, and must have tramped over the Cuilcagh Mountains, and by by-roads at night, to reach Lough Key.

"*Tá m'athair agus mo mháthair scannraithe,*" she said in Irish.

She didn't wish to embarrass her parents, and knew full well that her father at least would understand English, so she hoped that the gunman would understand her statement of the obvious in Irish, that her parents were frightened.

"*Níl Gaeilge agam*," he replied, "I know very little Irish, they wouldn't have Irish in our schools. And how," he added, his curiosity getting the better of him, "do you come to know Irish?"

"I've been here a couple of years studying it," she explained, "and I've been in the Gaeltacht. We've very little food here," she added, keeping a tremor out of her voice with great effort, "we're eating at restaurants on shore. We've only breakfast stuff here, coffee and biscuits that sort of thing. Why don't you just leave us? We won't tell anyone." "D'you expect me to believe that? Now that I'm here I may as well get you to help me, you can bring me down the river to Shannon." "This is the Shannon."

"I mean the airport."

"We can't even go as far as Limerick," she explained.

"Well somewhere in Clare then."

Ulrich had heard Erika say that he didn't understand English so spoke only in German, to ask her what the unwelcome visitor wanted. As she explained briefly, the gunman interjected: "You heard me, and I'm in a hurry: get moving and take me down the river." "Look," Erika said, gaining confidence, "we can't move in the dark, for one thing we couldn't see the course markers, and for another, it's forbidden and would be noticed right away by other boats. We have to stay here 'til morning anyway."

The confrontation was developing slowly in Erika's favour, but the gunman was not prepared to give in or give up. To establish his authority on more than his pistol, he made a quick decision.

"OK you two," he pointed to Hania and Ulrich, "toilet, then get into those two bunks at the front. And stay there until I tell you to get up. And remember that this girl will pay for it if you try any funny business." Again Erika translated, Ulrich inwardly fuming but waiting with a blank stare lest he reveal his knowledge of English.

The parents complied, while Erika, fearful, asked, "What

about me?" "Sorry about this," the gunman replied, "but you're my guarantee that they won't try anything funny. And this,"—he patted his gun—"is my guarantee that *you* won't try anything funny. Now hand me down that fishing rod, from the side of the roof; no, better still, take off the reel and give it to me. And give me your torch."

Erika took down the rod and began pushing apart the rings which held the reel firmly to the shaft.

"Here, give it to me," the gunman ordered, when it was clear the rings weren't budging. Then suddenly: "No you don't, smarty pants. You thought you'd catch me. Just keep on at that yourself until you get that reel clear and hand it to me, but move slowly and only when I tell you."

Finally the rings slid along the cork facing of the rod-butt, and she reached out the reel full of monofilament to her captor. He held it in his left hand for a while, meditating. Then he stood with his back to the recess in the prow to which he had ordered Ulrich and Hania, and flicked glances back and forth from Erika to the curtain behind him. Breathing heavily and working with one hand, the other holding the pistol, he looped the monofilament round a variety of projections; cup-hooks in the galley space, clothes-hooks over the table where Erika was sitting, handles of presses; constructing an invisible web. Finally, he threaded the monofilament through the handle of a cup and balanced this on a shaky heap of pots and pans, delft and cutlery. Further unwindings from the fishing reel gave monofilament for the weaving of another web, a fence, blocking the way to the short companionway and leaving Erika thus isolated in the central saloon. This web too he furnished with a terminal alarm, and with the boat divided hermetically into three cells, he switched out the light and sat slouched in the wheelhouse, the pistol held loosely on his knees.

Erika's thoughts ran frantically ahead to what might happen next and she visualised the following morning's scene at the lock.

"Do you know," she called softly to the hijacker, "it takes all three of us to get the boat through a lock?"

"What do you mean?" he asked, as he switched on the torch and stood it on the step of the companionway.

"There'll be several boats going through at the same time," she explained, "and one of us has to steer and run the motor, the others have to handle the bow and stern warps to keep the boat steady in the rush of water." He did not reply and she continued, "If you stay below we could tell other crews or the lock keeper what has happened. If you go on deck to keep tabs on us you'll have to take off that ridiculous mask, what's it for anyway? You might as well give up now, and go away and leave us in peace." She was speaking more bravely than she felt. "We'd never recognise you again, if you just go away with your mask on."

"Shut up and go to sleep," was the best rejoinder he could manage, clearly worried by the morrow's problem. They had been masked during their assault on the barracks at Florencecourt, so that they would not be recognised, then or later, by the security forces, who might photograph them in action, or might already have photographs of them on file. But a masked figure seen among the crew of a holiday cruiser passing through a lock on the Upper Shannon shouted 'terrorist.' Whereas if he stayed below, holding one of the three Germans as hostage for the other two, those two, on deck, would be able to tell other crews or lock-keepers of the unwelcome visitor below. And they had never seen him before, and would never see him again and did not know who he was. With some apparent relief, he made a decision, pulled the mask off, switched off the torch, and went to sleep.

$$\boxed{\text{kiss}}$$

Erika, physically and emotionally exhausted, had fallen asleep, and would have a dream or a memory of a first kiss. $\boxed{\text{escap}}$

Summer dawn came early, and the gunman snapped awake when one of his alarms crashed. "Toilet, toilet," Hania called, questioning and urgent.

"OK," the gunman answered, but tightened his grip on the pistol.

She pawed her way through the slackening web of monofilament and was surprised to see him sitting unmasked in the wheel-
house. His fresh round face had the pink and white bloom of
youth, a downy unshaven growth matching his tousled fair hair.

Hania used the tiny WC and returned to her bunk.

"But he's so young," she whispered to Ulrich, "He can't be
more than seventeen. I know that face exactly, it is the same as my
little brother; furtive, hunted, but defiant. He was so small he
could pass under the wire and at night he used to go everywhere,
to our *vati* in the men's section, sometimes to bring him food,
sometimes to get food from him ... the guards were very capri-
cious, sometimes they would leave us a few days without food
though nobody died ... if we tried to complain they'd shout
about the extermination camps ... but that boy ... we are the Or-
angemen of eastern Europe ..."

"How do you mean?"

"That's what the Polish communists thought we were ... my
Vati was the younger son, and was no use as a farmer, so he left
the good land where Germans had been settled since two hundred and more years ago ... he went to the city and got a job in
an ordinary Polish shop ... we spoke Polish with our friends on
the street and only spoke German to our parents at home and
with my very bad accent ... went to a Polish school ... then the
war came and the German army conquered Poland and the General Governor made an order that Germans, the *Volksdeutschen*,
must register ... but my *vati* said that's only for the people out in
the country in the German communities, we're staying here
where we belong ... even when the German armies invaded Russia ... our school lasted a short while, half underground, but children started disappearing ... a child would ask teacher, 'Where's
Rachel?' and teacher would look at me and say with tightened
lips, 'Perhaps Hania would know,' ... eventually this got so bad
that I would go home crying and my father decided at last that he
would register us as *Volksdeutsche*, but later in the war the German
armies were passing back into the Reich ..."

"I know, I was there ..." "And when the Russians established a government they arrested all the *Volksdeutschen* they could find, and many of them had fled with the army, but we were a few months in the camp, until they got tired of hearing us explain that we had lived with our Polish neighbours in the city and only registered as *Volksdeutsche* for the children's sake and not for taking any Polish property, and when I read about the Troubles in the north of Ireland I knew exactly what they were all about, and that boy with the gun pointing at our daughter is just like my little brother, furtive and fearful but defiant."

> whorl

> mask

Erika too had been wakened by the falling pillar of cups and saucers and saw the gunman's uncovered face. Like her mother, she was surprised at his youth. And she too was reminded of another boy—what was his name? On the return from that school trip to a printing-works in a remote suburb, they had taken an unfamiliar *Straßenbahn* line. All their classmates had left the streetcar when, in the darkening evening, she and the boy—what was his name, Willi something?—realised the car had left the public tracks and with a grinding sharp curve was entering a cavernous depot at the end of the line and being taken out of service. Gruffly dismissed by the driver they stood holding hands in the dark strange district. Fifteen-year-old Erika was scared and fretful, but Willi guided her through unknown streets and alleys to her home district and familiar shops. He came with her to the door of the block where, she knew, her parents in the penthouse apartment were worrying about her absence, and in a sudden flood of relief she threw her arms around him and kissed him on the lips. He returned her embrace, hugging her bosom to his chest, then said good night and walked away. But she was still excited as she was reminded of that first kiss.

He must have been about seventeen, and he had been trying to look like an artist, but his attempt at a beard was soft and downy to her lips, just like that boy there, with his mask off, showing several days' unshaven growth. Dare she risk a flirtation with the gunman? *Notfall*... she had read on the bulkhead above the wheel; the remains of English and French versions were there too, with spaces where peel-off-stick-on lettering had fallen off, ... *emergen ... use onl ...* and ... *urgence ... Mod ... emp ...* They all referred to the small cylinder on a bracket beside the notice. It was a signal flare, and Erika wondered how it worked — if she could get close enough she could read the instructions in small print in the rest of the notice headed ... *brauchsanwe ...* Was there a trigger on it, did it explode into searing flame with a sudden bang or did it build up slowly from a hiss to a roar? A slow-starting flare would be useless as a weapon, but if it was sudden and she could get near it ...

There seemed to be nothing for it, for the Germans, but to enter into the spirit of a deadly game. Although the guidebook said the locks were tended at all daylight hours, prudence dictated that too early an arrival at the upper gate would raise eyebrows and call attention. They applied the old maxim — never be first in or last out — and idled gently towards the lock-gate, third in a row of four boats waiting to descend at about nine o'clock.

The lock-chamber's latest passage the previous evening had been downstream, so the tail-gate was open and the water level was that of the lower reach. A few boats had overnighted below the lock and were awaiting passage upstream. A shout called the attention of the lock-keeper to a distant boat chugging upstream towards the lock, and, unhurried, he left the tail-gate open and rested on the beam waiting for this latecomer too to enter the chamber before closing the tail-gate and cranking the heavy racks — opening the upstream, closing the downstream — to fill the chamber. All this took half an hour or so, an interval filled with greetings between crews, mutual compliments on the fine weather we're having, an occasional plop of lure and float as line was hopefully cast into placid water.

The gunman, on deck with his unwilling hosts, fretted at the delay. Last night, hidden in the dark of the cabin, with his targets outlined against the night sky, he had been in control. Now, with the pistol bulging in his trouser pocket, drawing the attention of every passer-by, it seemed; his mask gone, his unshaven face for all to see; and remember, he knew he was an idle threat, he knew he daren't shoot, he knew they knew he daren't shoot; he was surviving only on the sufferance of his victims. They had now turned the river itself into a weapon far more powerful than his pistol, for all the deadly cartridges pressed into the spring-loaded clip in its butt, and the handful of bullets still weighing down his pockets.

Eventually, the chamber filled, the upstream gates were slowly opened and the upstream craft motored by. The downstream boats entered the huge chamber, warps were tended, gates closed, racks closed and opened, the chamber slowly emptied as *Medusa* and the others dropped slowly down into the depth of the dark and massive masonry structure. When the tail-gate swung open throttles were opened too and the four boats, emerging into the sun, chugged downstream and dispersed, each politely giving generous private water-space to the others, the gunman sighed with relief, out of the public eye.

Some minutes later he called to Ulrich, who was standing at the wheel, "Here, I'm going to need your jacket."

Both of them looked at Erika, who was coiling ropes on the narrow outer deck.

"What is it?" she asked, in English.

"Tell him I need his jacket."

Erika complied, adding that he obviously wanted to get rid of the paramilitary gear. With a shrug of resignation, Ulrich took a hand off wheel and throttle and gestured towards the prow, indicating that he had to stay in control of the boat. When they reached a quiet, smooth stretch of water, he made a turn into a gap in the flanking reed beds and throttled back. As the boat slowed, he gestured again to the gunman, and quickly slipped one arm out of the sleeve of his leather jacket. The boat yawed and he grabbed the wheel again with the unsleeved hand.

"*Hier*," he said, English or German, beckoning to the gunman, who approached. Again taking his hand off the controls, Ulrich slipped his other arm out of its sleeve and as the gunman reached out to take the jacket, Ulrich tossed it suddenly over the gunman's head and pulled it firmly down over his shoulders. As the gunman struggled against his grip, the hefty German stiffened and flattened one hand, and with its rigid edge dealt a firm blow to the gunman's neck, just below his ear. The gunman's body collapsed as suddenly and as completely as a bursting balloon and fell in a heap to the deck. Ulrich stirred the inert form with his foot, but knew that his victim was dead. Just in time, he took the controls again, shifted to reverse and they backed clear of dangerous vegetation. Looking around, Ulrich saw waving reeds in the complete circle of his vision, and could not discern by what winding channel through the reeds they had by chance entered this quiet lagoon during his argument by gesture with the gunman. But off the marked course of buoys and perches they surely were, out of sight of the firm banks of the Shannon, and, he realised, out of sight of any other cruiser, for there was no boat to be seen but their own *Medusa,* its crew two frightened women and a soldier who had just killed for the first time in thirty years.

The soldier switched off the engine, drew in the painter which brought the dinghy close to the stern, and lifted the warm body of the gunman into it. Telling the women to hold station, he rowed away round the point of an out-reaching bed of the tall reeds. He returned about twenty minutes later, reboarded *Medusa,* tied the painter, restarted the engine, and slowly nosed the boat around the open water until he saw a break in the green wall of reeds and carefully rejoined the main navigation channel of the Shannon.

A few days later, they motored back to the hire-company's marina at Carrick, and with careless skill Ulrich brought *Medusa* smartly to a convenient space on the jetty, cutting power and letting her drift the last few yards. Erika tossed the bow warp to the company's agent on the hard, and he dropped a quick loop of the line over a wooden bollard.

"Had a good time?" he called.

"Oh great," captain Ulrich answered, "and wonderful weather."

"Any problems with the boat?"

"None at all—though I'm afraid we lost a lot of line off the fishing rod."

"Ah that doesn't matter at all, did you manage to catch anything?" "I caught a healthy jack pike and a few other things but I put them all back. I'm not very good at disgorging, that's what my daughter says the trick is called, and maybe they were dead when I put them back into the water."

"Ah sure you did very well, would you believe I've seen some Germans who hand back their boats with the heads of big ones they caught fastened over the front window of the wheel-house? Some people have no conscience. Nothing else to report? ... Your car is safely where you left it ... Have a pleasant journey home ..."

ea

****

There was a woman standing at the hatch in the public office as the sergeant passed through on his way to lunch, a handsome middle-aged woman in holiday dress; jeans and a tee-shirt, flip-flops, a coloured light scarf around her neck, a string bag hanging from her shoulder. She spoke Irish to the Guard on duty, but a strange accented Irish. He responded, though taken aback, and she laughed.

"I am sorry," she said, "it's been so many years. We get plenty of chance in Germany to practise our English, but not much for Irish."

"How come you know Irish then?" he asked.

"I studied here for several years, many years ago, I even spent time in the Gaeltacht, but it's so rusty." "Good for you, ma'am. And so what can we do for you, have you some problem?" was his next question.

"It's not really a problem, I'm afraid, it's a solution. You see my father is dead now, and I feel I should tell you what happened when I was a student in Ireland thirty years ago ..."

eat

Knock knock

A LIBRARIAN ON EVENING SUPERVISORY DUTY will be very unlucky if he or she does not find enough time for generous browsing, and the eye will light from time to time on items of interest in obscure journals awaiting their return to their places in cavernous bookstacks. Thus it was that I chanced upon the name of Matthew Dowling, subject of a query in a respected journal devoted to the history of optics and optical instruments. The editorial reply to the enquiry treated of a nineteenth-century Co. Mayo eccentric who … But I had better present the facts in a logically chained order, rather than in the haphazard order in which they came to me.

There was a photograph, a sepia-tinted but faded *carte de visite* of a man seated in the conventional don't-move attitude of early photographs; he leans against the back of his steadying chair, one foot is raised and placed on a steadying stool. And perhaps to keep his hands steady, they are grasping a piece of apparatus. It is more or less cuboid in shape, apparently polished and for all the world like a misbegotten pair of binoculars. There are twin eyepieces on one narrow end, and opposite them, where one might expect to see the objective lenses, there is a flat screen of ground glass. There is a slot between that screen and a retractable flap. The slot permits the insertion of a special kind of photographic print known as a stereo-pair. Sets of these prints, accompanying their viewing apparatus, were a popular drawing-room entertainment in Victorian times. I can provide these details because I know what the object is and own one which is exactly the same, bought for shillings in a junk-shop on the quays many years ago. It is a stereoscope, a later version, perfected in France about 1850 and finished in shiny mahogany and brass, of the device invented by Wheatstone in 1839.

The stereo-pair, a pasteboard bearing two near-identical images, was inserted in the slot, and viewed through the eyepieces, left
eye seeing a print of a photograph which had been made through
the left-hand lens of a double-lensed camera, right eye seeing a
corresponding right-hand camera view. The two combined in a
mental simulacrum of the three-dimensional view of the world
enjoyed by people endowed with fairly normal sight in both their
eyes.[1] Sets of such pairs covered subjects as diverse as Beauties of
Ireland, Glories of the Holy Land, The Great Exhibition, Castles
and Cathedrals of England. They amused and instructed our an-
cestors and must have been an important adjunct to the tourist
trade, forerunners of the mass-produced picture postcard as holiday souvenir.

Far from any tourist resort, in County Mayo, a similar apparatus was in the hands of Matthew Dowling, philomath, sceptical
enquirer after truth. Perhaps it was he who sat still, stereoscope in
hand, in that faded *carte de visite*? More likely some unnamed
friend of the French *savant* who perfected that particular form of
stereoscope.

FAIR DAY SHOW
Mr. Matthew Dowling, expositor of the physical sciences, will
demonstrate his remarkable discovery of Coloured Pictures, to
be seen by all at the Camera Obscure tent, Bohola, on Thurs-
day, April 29. Gentlemen will be expected to contribute to the
cost of the entertainment and the experiments.
WESTERN CHRONICLE, Ballina

And Matthew Dowling had as well, according to the published
account, another piece of optical apparatus and had proposed to
combine the two in a new appliance. The second piece of apparatus was a magic lantern: in it, light from a carefully ventilated

---

1 If the pictures dropped in the slot be transparent, they are viewed with the instrument directed
at a source of light; if they be opaque the flap is opened to permit light to fall upon them and be
reflected.

source was condensed by a large lens, then passed through a glass plate bearing an image, then through an objective or focusing lens to a screen on which an enlarged image would appear and be enjoyed by an audience. The image on the slide might be educational — astronomical subjects were available — or the equivalent of the political cartoon in a modern newspaper.[2] The invention of photography in the mid-nineteenth century, of course, made it possible to project before an audience images of persons and places drawn from real life.

Matthew Dowling addressed two problems, and knew that if he could solve these he would be able to produce the greatest show on earth. He proposed to project two images on the screen, using for this purpose an adaptation of the magic lantern, and he proposed that a second image be projected close by the first, to create the stereo effect. And so he had to make it possible for members of an audience to view the double image as one viewed the double image in the stereoscope, the right eye seeing only a right-eye view, the left only a left-eye view.

Dowling enjoyed the collaboration of a fellow-enthusiast for the magic lantern. This was the local apothecary and his help was acknowledged both by Dowling and by the author of the note in the optics journal cited above. (Surely an unexpected coincidence — neighbours in a Co. Mayo village, far from centres of learning, with a common interest in what must have seemed to the other villagers something quite esoteric? But by such coincidences does science advance.)

For the first recorded experiment Dowling squintingly drew two pairs of images, each consisting of two circles, one within the other. (He traced the outlines of two coins, 1p and ½p.) In each

2 Pinhole versions of the magic lantern had been available for centuries as aids to draughtsmanship; in a darkened interior an image from a brightly illuminated exterior was cast, inverted, onto a screen by the passage of a narrow beam of light through a small hole, later augmented by a lens. There is no evidence that Dowling knew of the work of the Austrian, Baron von Uchatius, who, c.1853, successfully projected a series of phased drawings via magic lantern onto a screen where an illusion of continuous motion was achieved before a number of people (without, of course, the illusion of depth, relief or three-dimensionality). An article on the subject in the *National Encyclopaedia* (c. 1880) described the magic lantern as 'a species of lucernal microscope invented by Kirchner in 1645,' and concludes with the observation that 'The name given to the instrument is certainly most unfortunate.'

pair, the smaller one was placed slightly off-centre; and when these images were viewed in the stereoscope they did indeed present the three-dimensional image of one disc floating above another, a high-angle view of a half-penny-shape floating above a penny-shape, so to speak. This result convinced Dowling that the brain, given half a chance, would impose its idea of dimensionality on any object making the suggestion.

His collaborator now sacrificed his magic lantern in the cause of science and some special work followed which the published account does not describe in detail: the two magic lanterns were dismantled and reassembled with lights and lenses in a proximity which would (they hoped) cause the images to overlap to the degree necessary to sustain the illusion of relief or three-dimensionality.

Vain hope. Candles lit, condenser adjusted, light beam passing through slides (the disc outlines traced onto glass in Indian ink) — all they produced was a mess of wobbly lines on the screen, that is to say, on the white-washed wall of a nearby cottage.

"'Tis no good, Mattie," the friend is reported as saying, "them two images is interfering with one another. Don't you see we'll have to get one image to one of the eyes and th'other to th'other?"

The apothecary's mind ran readily to coloured bottles and he was prepared to make further sacrifices in the cause of science, so they cracked as carefully as they might a blue and a reddish-brown bottle from his stock, trimming pieces to fit into the paths of their light beams (and sanding their edges to bluntness after a few nasty cuts). Now left-eye views were projected through one colour, right-eye views through the other. And to compensate for the loss of light-intensity caused by interposition of the 'filters,' for the candles they substituted the more powerful illuminant of whale-oil lamps. Moreover, this time, no longer satisfied with simple discs floating over other discs, Dowling used tracings, outlines only, of a cut in the *Illustrated London News* depicting the cast of a popular London play.

Night fell, lamps were lit and trimmed, plates dropped into

slots, focus adjusted. And they beheld a murky reddish-blue mess of lines on the white wall across the street, which happened to be the wall of the parochial house.

"Mattie, boy," his friend said, after a pause, in an attempt to console the disappointed Dowling, "you know as well as I do the kinds of images you can get if you pass light reflected from an il-luminated object through a lens—real or virtual, erect or re-versed, enlarged or diminished, true or distorted? Well, the ones we're getting seem to be the distorted, and inverted, and they might be some use to our cousins in Van Diemen's Land or else-where in the far antipodes, but divil damn the use they are to us, boy, so we'll just have to go back and try something else."

There was this big wind one night and this man and woman had to go outside to see to the ass and the pigs they had in the haggard, because the pigs can see the wind you know, and as they came into the street they saw this light over the priest's house like a big lamp shining in the sky and they got the terrible fright for they never seen the like before and the man says to his wife, he says in Irish, An bhfeiceann tú é? *Do you see it? and* Feicim go maith, *I see it well, she says, and then the light swung around and lit up the side of the priest's house and got steady again and the man said,* An bhfeiceann tú anois é? *Do you see it now? and she says in her turn,* Feicim go breá soiléir é, *I see it right clearly, and when they carried on looking at the light, didn't it swing round again until it lit on the wall of the chapel, and what was it but a big big pic-ture of the Holy Family.* Ó a Thiarna Dia, *says the man,* an bh-feiceann tú anois é? *Do you see it now?* Feicim, *I do, says the woman back to him,* agus teanam go dtí an sagart anois, *let us go to the priest now and tell his reverence what we've seen, and they went and they told him about seeing the holy infant Jesus up there on the wall and His Blessed Mother and St. Joseph and all to that, and he told them to stay quiet about it until he'd made enquiry of the bishop, and that maybe only them could see it that had been to confession to get their sins forgiven and had received*

holy communion, and that's the way it's been to this very day,[3]
agus sin é mo scéalsa agus má tá bréag ann bíodh*, and that's my
story and if there's a word of a lie in it be it so.*
—IRISH FOLKLORE COMMISSION, SCHOOL SURVEY, 1932,
CO. MAYO, PARISH OF BÉAL A'CHOMHRAICAODÁN O CLÉIRIGH,
INFORMANT, AGE 73

Fr. Moran assured the congregation from the pulpit on his return
from Rome that he had been able to advise the Holy Father that
the faithful continued to flock to the site of the miraculous apparition of the Holy Family. "In 1854," he said, "the Blessed Mother
of God appeared to the humble St. Bernadette at Lourdes to
make manifest Divine approval of the doctrine of the Immaculate
Conception, then recently proclaimed by the Holy Father. '*Yo
soy*,' she said, speaking in the simple langue d'oc dialect of the locality, 'I am.' 'I am the Immaculate Conception.' As some of us
would say '*Is mise Muire a geineadh gan smál.*' So here in Co.
Mayo in 1870 the Holy Family deigned to appear to God-fearing
people to show them they must accept what had just been handed down by the magisterium of the Church, the doctrine of Papal
infallibility. "And I can tell you, my dear people," he concluded,
"that I have been advised quietly by the Vatican press office that a
statement will soon be issued indicating that His Holiness has
graciously consented to visit here in the course of his forthcoming
visit to Ireland and to perform the ceremonies of dedication of
the wonderful new basilica we have built to commemorate the
miraculous visitation vouchsafed by the Holy Family to our humble village." Fr. Moran assured the Taoiseach, favourite native son
of more counties than anyone else in the *Guinness Book of Records*,
that public funds expended on the development of the airport
would be generously repaid by the volume of traffic which the airport would generate: business leaders from abroad encouraged to

3 Successful simulation of relief or 3D in drawn film was achieved by the Scottish animator
Norman MacLaren and demonstrated in a short film appropriately entitled *Now is the time to put
on your glasses*. Production of stereoscopic moving images, and their projection on a square ribbed
screen, without benefit of eyeglasses, was achieved by Soviet filmmakers c. 1955.

come by promotional agencies; Irish workers in Britain and Europe returning for holidays or to resume or continue work in Ireland; visitors of the less giddy sort, scholarly tourists coming to visit the Yeats country; pilgrims to climb the Reek and to visit the site of the famous apparition of 1870. And many of these passengers would prefer to use this airport rather than an airport in any other county.

Fr. Moran assured the reporter who asked about the one-man picket at the dedication ceremony that one man was all it represented. "There's always to be found some deranged agnostic anticlerical attention-seeker like that," he said, "with his ridiculous placard: 'apparition not miraculous what about my grandda?' I mean to say, this is a preposterous attempt at a so-called rational explanation of an obviously supernatural event. The faith of the Irish is proof against these naysayers, and the prayers of the faithful to the Infant Jesus and His Blessed Mother in this new basilica will ensure, as we learnt from the catechism in childhood, that the Divine assistance will always remain with us and that the gates of hell shall not prevail."

I had heard that in Britain motorcycle *aficionados* used to make use of abandoned war-time landing strips for indulging their passion for speeding but never imagined that I should have the opportunity to make use of an airport runway not yet commissioned to give my very ordinary family car its head.

The airport so diligently lobbied for and so carefully promoted by the parish priest was slow a-building and even slower in the fitting out. No facilities yet for planes or people, no lights or navigation aids, no lounges, no litter bins, no rest rooms nor restaurant, no customs hall nor customers; just a billion tonnes or so of tarmac aggregate poured over a mist-shrouded upland bog. The only access was via a slipway which meandered from the main Galway-Sligo road and on a whim I left that main road and drove zig after zag up to and into the mist. Quickly I found myself isolated within a circle of visibility perhaps two car lengths across, and I travelled with it bump after bump until suddenly I was driving silently on smooth runway. With increasing daring I accelerated slightly, then a little more, and was soon enjoying the silence and aloneness. I felt a bump, saw that it was no longer smooth tarmac disappearing under my front wheels, and knew I had left the runway. With my heart in my mouth I executed a U-turn and dashed back the mile I had measured in my first transit, feeling the tingle of adrenalin as I reached twenty-five, and finally all of thirty m.p.h., still shrouded in that silver-grey enclosing fog. For a moment, I wished for wings and the sensation of lift, but reality triumphed and I braked successfully and found my way again to the main road.

I was exhilarated by this mad escapade and drove to the nearby town, where I found that even if that airport was not up and running, pilgrims were managing to reach the place in busloads. They wandered about the large open spaces—parking lots or church grounds—or knelt praying in front of the commemorative Marian shrine.

The shrine, in the open air, consisted of a group of life-size statues before a preserved fragment of the old wall on which the heavenly light reportedly played in 1870. The whole was encased in glass and set incongruously against the breeze-block wall of the new basilica, a building hard to distinguish from an advance factory in an industrial estate.

The pilgrims fingered their beads as they knelt before this shrine, or entered the basilica for other devotions. I left them to their orisons and dropped into a convenience store to pick up my newspaper. Convenient or not, it sold sweets, cigarettes, daily papers and the local weeklies, and for the rest was given over almost entirely to the traditional stock of the Catholic repository. Rosaries, of course; crucifixes and holy water fonts of various sizes to suit every room and purse; holy medals; holy pictures, small for your prayer book, or large framed jobs for your bedroom; hymnals; missals; other prayer books for young and old; Keys of Heaven; Gardens of the Soul; scapulars; Agnus Deis (if that's the correct plural); globular glass paperweights revealing, with a shake, a representation of snow falling on a tiny model of the new basilica; tall bottles containing bare crucifixes surrounded by other instruments of the Passion, ladder, hammer, towel. Less than traditional were the CDs and cassettes of sacred song by enthusiastic choirs, DVDs of visits to holy places, Beauraing, Kerrytown, Garabandal and Oberammergau among them, and Stations of the Cross in a Superman-comic-style booklet, complete with bubbles of talk and thought.

And this thingamajig in pink and white plastic, for all the world like a toy binoculars. I picked it up and put my eyes to what were obviously eyepieces but saw nothing until I pointed it at the light. Then I saw, in clear relief or 3D or stereoscopic simulation of depth, the conventional representation of the grotto at Lourdes, which graces the grounds of a thousand churches, convents and monasteries throughout Ireland — Bernadette kneeling before the blue-and-white-garbed Virgin Mary, a scroll above the Virgin's head bearing her declaration in langue d'oc that she is the Immaculate Conception.

I clicked an inviting little trigger on the side of the apparatus and other images came into view. They were the product of pairs of small transparencies (they looked like frames cut from 16mm film) set on the outer edge of a disc rotated by that trigger. They showed Lourdes, Medugorje, Garabandal, Beauraing, Fatima, and our own native apparition of 1870.

As to the nature of the images, never mind their subject, the illusion of depth or relief was totally convincing. Old Mattie would have been delighted. He had tried hard and very nearly made it. His very failure had passed into folklore and a scheming cleric, hiding rustic deviousness under the guise of a simple country priest, had finally turned it to account.

Bibliography, Sources

BERKELEY Geo., bp. of Cloyne, *An essay on a new theory of vision*. Dublin, 1708

CHANDLER Edward, *Photography in Ireland in the Nineteenth Century*. Dublin, 2004

EGAN Rev. Bartholemew, *Anecdotes from Tuam and Killala*. Westport, 1976 [largely, but not entirely, extracts from the author's voluminous diocesan histories]

EYE Journal of the Society for the Study of Optics and the History of Optical Instruments. [Vol.43, no. 2, spring, 1988, contains the original query concerning Matthew Dowling; vol. 44, no. 3, autumn, 1989, contains the response commissioned by the editor. The response is subscribed VB, generally held to be a pseudonym for a prominent Dublin ophthalmologist.]

KIRCHER R.P.A., *Athanasii Kircheri Ars Magna Lucis et Umbrae, in X libro digesta, ...* Amsterdam, 1671 ["... *une véritable encyclopédie des connaissances optiques ...*" A note elsewhere states "*Les appareils optiques du XVIIIe siècle étaient d'une excellente construction et la « camera obscura » donnait des images parfaites, qui ont fait rêver les artistes et stimulé les imaginations.*" Dowling, however, was more likely to have been influenced, if at all, by the achievement of Philipsthal who, in London, in 1802, projected images onto one side of a transparent screen so that spectators on the other side "could scarcely divest themselves of the idea that they were looking into a dark cavern, in which the objects appeared to be gradually approaching towards or receding from them." (*National Encyclopaedia*)]

LARKIN Emmet, *The Devotional Revolution: the Roman Catholic Church in Late Nineteenth-Century Ireland*. Chicago, 1978

POCHIN-MOULD Daphne, *Ireland's holy places*. Cork, 1963

SWIFT Jonathan, D.S.P.D., *The magick lanthorn as beamed upon Dr. A-b-t-n-t in a late session of parliament*. Dublin, 1718 [I have not seen this work, which is unknown to Teerink, and the attribution is at least doubtful. The title may have nothing to do with the apparatus of which we treat, and may be merely one of those coincidences which can be the means of advancing knowledge.]

Personal communications

MICHAL AJVAZ, *The Golden Age.*
The Other City.

PIERRE ALBERT-BIROT, *Grabinoulor.*

YUZ ALESHKOVSKY, *Kangaroo.*

FELIPE ALFAU, *Chromos. Locos.*

IVAN ÂNGELO, *The Celebration.*
The Tower of Glass.

ANTÓNIO LOBO ANTUNES, *Knowledge
of Hell.*
The Splendor of Portugal.

ALAIN ARIAS-MISSON, *Theater of Incest.*

JOHN ASHBERY & JAMES SCHUYLER,
A Nest of Ninnies.

ROBERT ASHLEY, *Perfect Lives.*

GABRIELA AVIGUR-ROTEM, *Heatwave
and Crazy Birds.*

DJUNA BARNES, *Ladies Almanack.*
Ryder.

JOHN BARTH, *Letters.*
Sabbatical.

DONALD BARTHELME, *The King.*
Paradise.

SVETISLAV BASARA, *Chinese Letter.*

MIQUEL BAUÇÀ, *The Siege in the Room.*

RENÉ BELLETTO, *Dying.*

MAREK BIENCZYK, *Transparency.*

ANDREI BITOV, *Pushkin House.*

ANDREJ BLATNIK, *You Do Understand.*

LOUIS PAUL BOON, *Chapel Road.*
My Little War.
Summer in Termuren.

ROGER BOYLAN, *Killoyle.*

IGNÁCIO DE LOYOLA BRANDÃO, *Zero.*
Anonymous Celebrity.

BONNIE BREMSER, *Troia: Mexican
Memoirs.*

CHRISTINE BROOKE-ROSE,
Amalgamemnon.

BRIGID BROPHY, *In Transit.*

GERALD L. BRUNS, *Modern Poetry and
the Idea of Language.*

GABRIELLE BURTON, *Heartbreak Hotel.*

MICHEL BUTOR, *Degrees. Mobile.*

G. CABRERA INFANTE, *Infante's Inferno.*
Three Trapped Tigers.

ARNO CAMENISCH, *The Alp.*

JULIETA CAMPOS, *The Fear of Losing
Eurydice.*

ANNE CARSON, *Eros the Bittersweet.*

ORLY CASTEL-BLOOM, *Dolly City.*

LOUIS-FERDINAND CÉLINE, *North.*
Rigadoon.
Castle to Castle.
Conversations with Professor Y.
London Bridge.
Normance.

MARIE CHAIX, *The Laurels of Lake
Constance.*

HUGO CHARTERIS, *The Tide Is Right.*

ERIC CHEVILLARD, *Demolishing Nisard.*

MARC CHOLODENKO, *Mordechai
Schamz.*

JOSHUA COHEN, *Witz.*

EMILY HOLMES COLEMAN, *The Shutter
of Snow.*

ROBERT COOVER, *A Night at the Movies.*

STANLEY CRAWFORD, *Log of the S.S.
The Mrs Unguentine.*
Some Instructions to My Wife.

S.D. CHROSTOWSKA, *Permission.*

RENÉ CREVEL, *Putting My Foot in It.*

RALPH CUSACK, *Cadenza.*

NICHOLAS DELBANCO, *Sherbrookes.*
The Count of Concord.

NIGEL DENNIS, *Cards of Identity.*

PETER DIMOCK, *A Short Rhetoric for
Leaving the Family.*

ARIEL DORFMAN, *Konfidenz.*

COLEMAN DOWELL, *Island People.*
Too Much Flesh and Jabez.

ARKADII DRAGOMOSHCHENKO,
Dust.

RIKKI DUCORNET, *Phosphor in
Dreamland.*
The Complete Butcher's Tales.
The Jade Cabinet.
The Fountains of Neptune.

WILLIAM EASTLAKE, *The Bamboo Bed.*
Castle Keep.
Lyric of the Circle Heart.
JEAN ECHENOZ, *Chopin's Move.*
STANLEY ELKIN, *A Bad Man.*
Criers and Kibitzers, Kibitzers and Criers.
The Dick Gibson Show.
The Franchiser.
The Living End.
Mrs. Ted Bliss.
FRANÇOIS EMMANUEL, *Invitation to a Voyage.*
SALVADOR ESPRIU, *Ariadne in the Grotesque Labyrinth.*
LESLIE A. FIEDLER, *Love and Death in the American Novel.*
JUAN FILLOY, *Op Oloop.*
ANDY FITCH, *Pop Poetics.*
GUSTAVE FLAUBERT, *Bouvard and Pécuchet.*
KASS FLEISHER, *Talking out of School.*
JON FOSSE, *Aliss at the Fire.*
Melancholy.
FORD MADOX FORD, *The March of Literature.*
MAX FRISCH, *I'm Not Stiller.*
Man in the Holocene.
CARLOS FUENTES, *Adam in Eden.*
Christopher Unborn.
Distant Relations.
Terra Nostra.
Where the Air Is Clear.
TAKEHIKO FUKUNAGA, *Flowers of Grass.*
WILLIAM GADDIS, JR., *The Recognitions.*
JANICE GALLOWAY, *Foreign Parts.*
The Trick Is to Keep Breathing.
WILLIAM H. GASS, *Cartesian Sonata and Other Novellas.*
The Tunnel. Willie Masters' Lonesome Wife.
GÉRARD GAVARRY, *Hoppla! 1 2 3.*
ETIENNE GILSON, *The Arts of the Beautiful.*
Forms and Substances in the Arts.

C. S. GISCOMBE, *Giscome Road.*
Here.
DOUGLAS GLOVER, *Bad News of the Heart.*
WITOLD GOMBROWICZ, *A Kind of Testament.*
PAULO EMÍLIO SALES GOMES, *P's Three Women.*
GEORGI GOSPODINOV, *Natural Novel.*
JUAN GOYTISOLO, *Count Julian.*
Juan the Landless.
Makbara.
Marks of Identity.
HENRY GREEN, *Back.*
Blindness.
Concluding.
Doting.
Nothing.
JACK GREEN, *Fire the Bastards!*
JIŘÍ GRUŠA, *The Questionnaire.*
MELA HARTWIG, *Am I a Redundant Human Being?*
JOHN HAWKES, *The Passion Artist.*
Whistlejacket.
ELIZABETH HEIGHWAY, ED., *Contemporary Georgian Fiction.*
ALEKSANDAR HEMON, ED., *Best European Fiction.*
AIDAN HIGGINS, *Balcony of Europe.*
Blind Man's Bluff.
Bornholm Night-Ferry.
Flotsam and Jetsam.
Langrishe, Go Down.
Scenes from a Receding Past.
KEIZO HINO, *Isle of Dreams.*
KAZUSHI HOSAKA, *Plainsong.*
ALDOUS HUXLEY, *Antic Hay.*
Crome Yellow.
Point Counter Point.
Those Barren Leaves.
Time Must Have a Stop.
NAOYUKI II, *The Shadow of a Blue Cat.*
GERT JONKE, *Awakening to the Great Sleep War.*
The Distant Sound.

GERT JONKE (cont.), *Geometric Regional Novel.*
Homage to Czerny.
The System of Vienna.
JACQUES JOUET, *Mountain R. Savage.*
Upstaged.
MIEKO KANAI, *The Word Book.*
YORAM KANIUK, *Life on Sandpaper.*
HUGH KENNER, *Flaubert.*
Joyce and Beckett: The Stoic Comedians.
Joyce's Voices.
DANILO KIŠ, *The Attic.*
Garden, Ashes.
The Lute and the Scars.
Psalm 44.
A Tomb for Boris Davidovich.
ANITA KONKKA, *A Fool's Paradise.*
GEORGE KONRÁD, *The City Builder.*
TADEUSZ KONWICKI, *A Minor Apocalypse.*
The Polish Complex.
MENIS KOUMANDAREAS, *Koula.*
ELAINE KRAF, *The Princess of 72nd Street.*
JIM KRUSOE, *Iceland.*
AYSE KULIN, *Farewell: A Mansion in Occupied Istanbul.*
EMILIO LASCANO TEGUI, *On Elegance While Sleeping.*
ERIC LAURRENT, *Do Not Touch.*
VIOLETTE LEDUC, *La Bâtarde.*
EDOUARD LEVÉ, *Autoportrait.*
Suicide.
Works.
MARIO LEVI, *Istanbul Was a Fairy Tale.*
DEBORAH LEVY, *Billy and Girl.*
JOSÉ LEZAMA LIMA, *Paradiso.*
ROSA LIKSOM, *Dark Paradise.*
OSMAN LINS, *Avalovara.*
The Queen of the Prisons of Greece.
ALF MAC LOCHLAINN, *Out of Focus.*
The Corpus in the Library.
RON LOEWINSOHN, *Magnetic Field(s).*
MINA LOY, *Stories and Essays of Mina Loy.*
J.M. MACHADO DE ASSIS, *Stories.*

MELISSA MALOUF, *More Than You Know.*
D. KEITH MANO, *Take Five.*
MICHELINE AHARONIAN MARCOM, *The Mirror in the Well.*
A Brief History of Yes.
BEN MARCUS, *The Age of Wire and String.*
WALLACE MARKFIELD, *Teitlebaum's Window.*
To an Early Grave.
DAVID MARKSON, *Reader's Block.*
Wittgenstein's Mistress.
CAROLE MASO, *AVA.*
LADISLAV MATEJKA & KRYSTYNA POMORSKA, EDS., *Readings in Russian Poetics: Formalist and Structuralist Views.*
HARRY MATHEWS, *Cigarettes.*
The Conversions.
The Human Country: New and Collected Stories.
The Journalist.
My Life in CIA.
Singular Pleasures.
The Sinking of the Odradek.
Stadium.
Tlooth.
JOSEPH MCELROY, *Night Soul and Other Stories.*
DONAL MCLAUGHLIN, *beheading the virgin mary.*
ABDELWAHAB MEDDEB, *Talismano.*
GERHARD MEIER, *Isle of the Dead.*
HERMAN MELVILLE, *The Confidence-Man.*
AMANDA MICHALOPOULOU, *I'd Like.*
STEVEN MILLHAUSER, *The Barnum Museum.*
In the Penny Arcade.
RALPH J. MILLS, JR., *Essays on Poetry.*
MOMUS, *The Book of Jokes.*
CHRISTINE MONTALBETTI, *The Origin of Man.*
Western.
OLIVE MOORE, *Spleen.*

NICHOLAS MOSLEY, *Accident.*
Assassins.
Catastrophe Practice.
Experience and Religion.
A Garden of Trees.
Hopeful Monsters.
Imago Bird.
Impossible Object.
Inventing God.
Judith.
Look at the Dark.
Natalie Natalia.
Serpent.
Time at War.

WARREN MOTTE, *Fables of the Novel: French Fiction since 1990.*
Fiction Now: The French Novel in the 21st Century.
Oulipo: A Primer of Potential Literature.

GERALD MURNANE, *Barley Patch.*
Inland.

YVES NAVARRE, *Our Share of Time.*
Sweet Tooth.

DOROTHY NELSON, *In Night's City.*
Tar and Feathers.

ESHKOL NEVO, *Homesick.*

WILFRIDO D. NOLLEDO, *But for the Lovers.*

FLANN O'BRIEN, *At Swim-Two-Birds.*
The Best of Myles.
The Dalkey Archive.
The Hard Life.
The Poor Mouth.
The Third Policeman.

CLAUDE OLLIER, *The Mise-en-Scène.*
Wert and the Life Without End.

GIOVANNI ORELLI, *Walaschek's Dream.*

PATRIK OUŘEDNÍK, *Europeana.*
The Opportune Moment, 1855.

BORIS PAHOR, *Necropolis.*

FERNANDO DEL PASO, *News from the Empire.*
Palinuro of Mexico.

ROBERT PINGET, *The Inquisitory.*
Mahu or The Material.
Trio.

MANUEL PUIG, *Betrayed by Rita Hayworth.*
The Buenos Aires Affair.
Heartbreak Tango.

RAYMOND QUENEAU, *The Last Days.*
Odile.
Pierrot Mon Ami.
Saint Glinglin.

ANN QUIN, *Berg.*
Passages.
Three.
Tripticks.

ISHMAEL REED, *The Free-Lance Pallbearers.*
The Last Days of Louisiana Red.
Ishmael Reed: The Plays.
Juice!
Reckless Eyeballing.
The Terrible Threes.
The Terrible Twos.
Yellow Back Radio Broke-Down.

JASIA REICHARDT, *15 Journeys Warsaw to London.*

NOËLLE REVAZ, *With the Animals.*

JOÃO UBALDO RIBEIRO, *House of the Fortunate Buddhas.*

JEAN RICARDOU, *Place Names.*

RAINER MARIA RILKE, *The Notebooks of Malte Laurids Brigge.*

JULIÁN RÍOS, *The House of Ulysses.*
Larva: A Midsummer Night's Babel.
Poundemonium.
Procession of Shadows.

AUGUSTO ROA BASTOS, *I the Supreme.*

DANIËL ROBBERECHTS, *Arriving in Avignon.*

JEAN ROLIN, *The Explosion of the Radiator Hose.*

OLIVIER ROLIN, *Hotel Crystal.*

ALIX CLEO ROUBAUD, *Alix's Journal.*

JACQUES ROUBAUD, *The Form of a City Changes Faster, Alas, Than the Human Heart.*
The Great Fire of London.
Hortense in Exile.
Hortense is Abducted.

FOR A FULL LIST OF PUBLICATIONS, VISIT: www.dalkeyarchive.com

JACQUES ROUBAUD (cont.), *The Loop.*
 Mathematics: The Plurality of Worlds of Lewis.
 The Princess Hoppy.
 Some Thing Black.
RAYMOND ROUSSEL,
 Impressions of Africa.
VEDRANA RUDAN, *Night.*
STIG SÆTERBAKKEN, *Siamese.*
 Self Control.
 Through the Night.
LYDIE SALVAYRE, *The Company of Ghosts.*
 The Lecture.
 The Power of Flies.
LUIS RAFAEL SÁNCHEZ, *Macho Camacho's Beat.*
SEVERO SARDUY, *Cobra & Maitreya.*
NATHALIE SARRAUTE, *Do You Hear Them?*
 Martereau.
 The Planetarium.
ARNO SCHMIDT, *Collected Novellas.*
 Collected Stories.
 Nobodaddy's Children.
 Two Novels.
ASAF SCHURR, *Motti.*
GAIL SCOTT, *My Paris.*
DAMION SEARLS,
 What We Were Doing and Where We Were Going.
JUNE AKERS SEESE, *Is This What Other Women Feel Too?*
 What Waiting Really Means.
BERNARD SHARE, *Inish. Transit.*
VIKTOR SHKLOVSKY, *Bowstring.*
 Knight's Move.
 A Sentimental Journey: Memoirs 1917–1922.
 Energy of Delusion: A Book on Plot.
 Literature and Cinematography.
 Theory of Prose.
 Third Factory.
 Zoo, or Letters Not about Love.
PIERRE SINIAC, *The Collaborators.*
KJERSTI A. SKOMSVOLD, *The Faster I Walk, the Smaller I am.*

JOSEF ŠKVORECKÝ,
 The Engineer of Human Souls.
GILBERT SORRENTINO, *Aberration of Starlight.*
 Blue Pastoral.
 Crystal Vision.
 Imaginative Qualities of Actual Things.
 Mulligan Stew.
 Pack of Lies.
 Red the Fiend.
 The Sky Changes.
 Something Said.
 Splendide-Hôtel.
 Steelwork.
 Under the Shadow.
W. M. SPACKMAN, *The Complete Fiction.*
ANDRZEJ STASIUK, *Dukla.*
 Fado.
GERTRUDE STEIN, *The Making of Americans.*
 A Novel of Thank You.
GWEN LI SUI (ED.), *Telltale: 11 Stories.*
LARS SVENDSEN, *A Philosophy of Evil.*
PIOTR SZEWC, *Annihilation.*
GONÇALO M. TAVARES, *Jerusalem.*
 Joseph Walser's Machine.
 Learning to Pray in the Age of Technique.
LUCIAN DAN TEODOROVICI, *Our Circus Presents ...*
NIKANOR TERATOLOGEN, *Assisted Living.*
STEFAN THEMERSON, *Hobson's Island.*
 The Mystery of the Sardine.
 Tom Harris.
TAEKO TOMIOKA, *Building Waves.*
JOHN TOOMEY, *Sleepwalker.*
JEAN-PHILIPPE TOUSSAINT,
 The Bathroom.
 Camera.
 Monsieur.
 Reticence.
 Running Away.
 Self-Portrait Abroad.
 Television.
 The Truth about Marie.

DUMITRU TSEPENEAG, *Hotel Europa.*
The Necessary Marriage.
Pigeon Post.
Vain Art of the Fugue.

ESTHER TUSQUETS, *Stranded.*

DUBRAVKA UGRESIC,
Lend Me Your Character.
Thank You for Not Reading.

TOR ULVEN, *Replacement.*

MATI UNT, *Brecht at Night.*
Diary of a Blood Donor.
Things in the Night.

ÁLVARO URIBE & OLIVIA SEARS, EDS.,
Best of Contemporary Mexican Fiction.

ELOY URROZ, *Friction.*
The Obstacles.

BUKET UZUNER, *I am Istanbul.*

LUISA VALENZUELA, *Dark Desires and
the Others.*
He Who Searches.

PAUL VERHAEGHEN, *Omega Minor.*

AGLAJA VETERANYI, *Why the Child is
Cooking in the Polenta.*

BORIS VIAN, *Heartsnatcher.*

LLORENÇ VILLALONGA, *The Dolls'
Room.*

TOOMAS VINT, *An Unending Landscape.*

IGOR VISHNEVETSKY, *Leningrad.*

ORNELA VORPSI, *The Country Where No
One Ever Dies.*

AUSTRYN WAINHOUSE, *Hedyphagetica.*

CURTIS WHITE, *America's Magic
Mountain.*
The Idea of Home.
Memories of My Father Watching TV.
Requiem.

DIANE WILLIAMS, *Excitability:
Selected Stories.*
Romancer Erector.

DOUGLAS WOOLF, *Wall to Wall.*
Ya! & John-Juan.

JAY WRIGHT, *Polynomials and Pollen.*
The Presentable Art of Reading Absence.

PHILIP WYLIE, *Generation of Vipers.*

MARGUERITE YOUNG, *Angel in
the Forest.*
Miss MacIntosh, My Darling.

REYOUNG, *Unbabbling.*

VLADO ŽABOT, *The Succubus.*

ZORAN ŽIVKOVIĆ , *Hidden Camera.*

LOUIS ZUKOFSKY, *Collected Fiction.*

VITOMIL ZUPAN, *Minuet for Guitar.*

SCOTT ZWIREN, *God Head.*